RELICS

from the Underworld

by

Richard Alan Scott

Crystal Lake Publishing
www.CrystalLakePub.com

Torrid Waters is the pulp and extreme horror imprint of Crystal Lake Entertainment. For this book, the author has supplied the following trigger warnings: violence, murder, paranormal malevolence.

Prelude

Petrograd, USSR, February 1922

"If the nobles, aristocrats, destroy me, then their hands will be stained with my blood and they will leave Russia. King of the Russian land, if you hear a bell ringing that tells you Grigori has been killed, know that one of yours set up my death and none of you, none of your children will live more than two years… Russian Tsar, you will be killed by the Russian people, and the people themselves will be cursed to become instruments of the Devil."

This prediction of Father Grigori Rasputin, from a 1916 letter, was read aloud by Lenin's recently appointed secretary general of the newly formed USSR, Josef Stalin. He would become one of history's great sociopaths.

The secretary was opening the ceremonies of an underground auction being held at the site of the Winter Palace. Only the most elite and consequential of Europe had been summoned, as there was no official pronouncement of said auction taking place. They would bid on remnants of the Bolshevik Revolution of 1917.

This may have included former Russian nobility, deep in disguise.

No passers-by would discern the purpose behind the swarm of Barker Limousines parked outside. The weird holy man's visions about his and the royal family's assassinations would set the perfect tone for bidding on the powerful occult items, in what would surely be a bizarre night.

Even the leader of Germany's newly recognized Nazi Party, a decorated war hero, was in attendance. He would also become one of history's great sociopaths.

1. The Black Banana

Tatiana felt invisible at Holcomb and Brown. At thirty, she was still just a mousy thing from her tightly wound bun to her sensible Doc Martins, her voice rarely rising above a whisper. She wore contacts now, but she'd worn glasses before that. Without one or the other, her eyes would narrow into squinty slits, and she couldn't see much.

"God, Ana. Can't you use part of that inheritance to buy new outfits, some shoes?" her assistant, Angie scolded. A Bronx Italian and a bit younger than Tatiana, Angie always concerned herself too much with the fact that Tatiana's appearance evoked titters from the other administrative aides. "And sweety, get your hair done. There's nothing special about looking like a homeless waif, you know?"

She had a point. Tatiana did want to be noticed. Angie often caught her staring longingly at Stephen, her fellow account manager.

"Listen to Auntie Angie, babe. Forget about yummy Steve. I'd bet your windfall he's got a rich fiancée in the Hamptons. Now, if you take my makeover advice, and we go out Friday—" The ceaseless ringing that ruled their lives had cut her off.

Tatiana instantly returned to her ogling. She'd rather daydream of Stephen's dark curls and piercing blue eyes. Besides, she was stumped for an idea on her assigned ad campaign, an original approach for the Lumos Company, designers of home lighting.

"It's that creepy French guy again," Angie said. "He always says it's urgent."

"I'll take it in my office. Thanks, Angie." Tatiana picked up her own receiver behind closed doors. "*Bonjour, Monsieur. Comment allez-vous?*"

"*Ah, tres bien, merci, Mademoiselle Tati.*" Louis Martelle was a dealer of rare antiquities—both a passion and addiction of Tatiana's.

"Are you sitting down for the news I have for you?"

A jolt of electricity went through her belly, and a premonition overtook her. "You didn't…? You don't…have *it*?"

"*Oui*, you are psychic, *Mademoiselle*. I do indeed have in my possession the artifact you have yearned for these many years. With your sponsorship and generous offer for my commission, I was able to procure it at auction today."

"But how? How in the world, Louis? I thought it was tied up at the museum in St. Petersburg?"

"Ah," he answered. "It seems there is not much interest in erotic exhibits, even in the new forward-thinking Russia. Alas, the museum is going under, and the doctor is desperate for offers like yours. Now, I am in New York; should I drop by with your merchandise tonight, say seven thirty, *Mademoiselle Tati?*"

Tatiana had tears in her eyes. She had to wipe saliva from her lips. "*Absolument, Monsieur.* I will see you then." Tatiana put down the receiver.

As if seeing the light on the phone go off, Angie announced through the speaker, "Your uncle is on line two, Ana. He's been waiting."

"Thanks," Tatiana said. She picked up the phone again and hit the blinking light. "Hello, Stasi."

"Hello, *malyutka*. And please don't call me that. You know how I feel..."

Tatiana only giggled. Uncle Stasya was her only living relative, and the dearest soul in the world. "Then don't call me your child, Uncle. I may not act it, but I'm a grown woman." She laughed again to show she was teasing.

"You seem in a pleasant state," he said. "Is there something or someone I should know about?"

"Oh, just the greatest Russian antiquities score of my life," she admitted. "I am overwhelmingly excited."

"Aach, to waste your grandmother's money on such things!" said Stasya. "I don't know why you want to wallow in the past. Your mother and I were lucky to have gotten out of that place, *Khristos* preserve her. I will be putting my cut of *Babushka's* riches into stocks, so that they may make more riches."

"Good for you," Tatiana teased. "But to me, the past is made of riches, riches worth more than gold."

"Speaking of money, I have to warn you." Stasya's tone grew serious. "I've heard from my friend that he's worried about you. He says you had some promising ideas at the outset, but that you have dried up for months. He says you have cost them some valuable clients. I think if you don't produce some advertising genius soon, especially on this Lumos account, it may be back to waitressing for you."

"Brodchke is an old fuddy-duddy." She pouted. "I try, but he never likes my ideas. He'll pick a man's campaign over mine every time."

"Mister *Brown* has been more than generous in repaying the favor he owed me. Perhaps you should begin to think like a man. I'm afraid time is running out on you. Enjoy your acquisition tonight but come in tomorrow with your head in the game." He no longer sounded tolerant. "I have to go; you know I love you."

"I promise, Uncle. I love you too." Tatiana was momentarily upset as she put the receiver down. Then she thought of what was coming tonight, and the cares of work didn't matter.

The Rasputin family lived in a small village named Pokrovskoye on the remote steppes of Siberia. Grigori, a peasant boy who would grow to mingle with Russian royalty, was gifted with strange powers even as a child. It was said he could communicate with animals and heal them. Being clairvoyant, he knew when someone in the village would die. His constant companion was his brother, Mikhail.

Grischa and Mischa, always together.

When Grischa turned eight and Mischa ten, they went swimming in the Tura River. Mischa went in first. When he tried to stand, he ended up over a sinkhole and had nowhere to settle against the current. Grischa tried to pull him out but was pulled in instead. The current dragged them quite a way until a passing farmer pulled them out.

Both boys developed pneumonia. Only Grischa got better.

It was said that Grischa's psychic power, as celebrated as it later became, was never again as powerful as before Mischa's death.

Rae-Ann stood outside Tatiana's door in their apartment building, her only true friend outside of work. She knocked at eight-thirty that evening, after her shift as restaurant hostess ended. As always, she walked right in without an answer, just like Tatiana had instructed.

"Tatiana," Rae-Ann called out, not seeing her immediately. The living room was a giant mess of torn cardboard and white Styrofoam packing peanuts. The place had been cluttered enough with Tatiana's junk collection from her native Russia. Tatiana had bayonets and pieces of armor on the wall, ornate jewel-encrusted eggs and nesting dolls all over the mantle and tables. Her friend was especially proud of her religious icons, which, in Rae-Ann's opinion, were too creepy for an apartment. There was no one quite like her geeky but lovable neighbor. Tatiana's vulnerable awkwardness brought out the nurturer in Rae-Ann.

"Tatiana," she called again.

"In here," came a reply from the bedroom, followed by, "brace yourself!"

Rae-Ann waded through the rubble to the hallway beyond the parlor, and then took a left into Tatiana's bedroom. "Oh my God, girl. What the fuck is that?" Rae-Ann was mortified. "Is that what I think it is?"

Tatiana sat on her bed, beaming from ear to ear. She was in her pajamas already and, as Rae-Ann approached, she quietly exclaimed, "Ta-daa!"

On the night table sat a large glass jar, about twenty inches high and six inches in diameter. It had an ornate top, held in place without being locked on. It was filled to fifteen inches with a clear fluid that looked more substantial than water. Standing in this liquid was an enormous, dismembered, dark male organ, complete with testes, scrotum, and part of the pubic area. Its tip was at the bottom of the jar and the top of the pubis was barely beneath the surface of the fluid.

Rae-Ann screamed in mock terror, and Tatiana delighted in her shock and amazement.

"Again, I say, what the fuck? I've seen some brothers with big-ass shit, but that takes the cake."

"My dear," Tatiana began as she composed herself, "you are in the presence of the last of Father Grigori Rasputin himself, the man who influenced the Czarina and cured the hemophiliac son of Czar Nicholas. You are seeing the most prominent remains of Czarist Russia."

"I'm seeing one hell of a dick!" Rae-Ann replied, and they both wailed. "You've collected some weird Russian shit girl, but come on now, you are one sick puppy."

"It's really true," Tatiana defended herself. "Do you realize how rare...how much this is worth? We're talking about 1916.

Rasputin was castrated by Prince Yusupova and his assassins. The story goes that a servant in Yusupova's house, a devoted admirer of Father Grigori's, spirited the relic away. Some royals fleeing the Revolution were then able to take it to America. I was fascinated after hearing of its existence from my grandmother, and my whole life I've been trying to get my hands on it."

"That's one way of putting it," joked Rae-Ann.

Tatiana smiled softly then got serious. "Do you know how long I've waited for this day, Rae? Rasputin has always been the most fascinating historical figure to me, and now I own a piece of him! I acquired it from a surgeon who ran a museum of erotica in St. Petersburg. You won't believe how much I paid for it."

"Please don't tell me, Tatiana. I know it'd make me sick. Hell, honey, if it floats your boat, more power to you. I'm happy."

Tatiana rose and threw her arms around Rae-Ann, who chuckled at the situation. They stood looking at the artifact.

"Well Father Grigori, or Mister Rasputin, it's a pleasure to make your acquaintance!" Rae-Ann said. Tatiana feigned slapping her arm. "You'll forgive me if I don't shake hands."

They laughed and embraced as Rae-Ann shook her head in disbelief.

Tatiana stirred in the darkness. She awoke bathed in sweat with her heart racing. Her head pounded.

Had she just heard a voice, or was it a dream? Her room was freezing, and it was so dark that it disoriented her. She remembered she had fallen asleep with a candle burning. It was unusual for it to go out while she slept; she bought long-burning pillars. A tremendous wind blew outside. Her window rattled, and a breeze came through the sides of the old sill.

Probably what blew the candle out.

It was too quiet outside for Manhattan. Usually, she heard a chorus of street sounds. The world seemed foreign somehow, like something odd was occurring. But what?

Still groggy, she rolled over to go back to sleep. But she caught a glimpse of her alarm clock; 3:33. The red light from the dial penetrated the fluid in the container on her bedstand and illuminated her new artifact. She stared at it until her eyes began to close. She stared at it like she had other things as a child, almost willing it to move.

And then it did.

No, you imagined it.

But the fluid; there were bubbles from the movement.

Okay, now I'm losing it. She closed her eyes and drifted off.

"*Moy malenki.*"

She jumped, her eyes springing open. This time she had heard something—a man's voice, deep and resonant. She was afraid. It wasn't like her; she considered herself a tough New Yorker. She ignored the instinct to investigate, instead cowering deeper into her comforter.

Weakly, her voice quavering, she said, "Uncle Stasi?" The man had said 'my little one,' which wasn't Stasi's usual endearment but close.

"Stasi?" she asked again, but the apartment remained silent.

She was just about convinced she'd imagined it when she saw him standing in her doorway, a silhouette. He was tall, imposing, and smelled of stale cologne and Vodka. Tatiana could make out unkempt long hair and a full beard. She lay helpless, terrified. She tried to ask what he wanted, but nothing came out.

"*Lyubovnik*," he said, which meant 'Lover.' The timbre of his voice had almost been soothing.

Tatiana wanted to scream, to rise and rush past him, to grab her cell phone and lock herself in the bathroom, but she did none of these things. She was paralyzed, could only lie there.

Then she heard herself speak, but it was as if the voice came from outside her. "*Lyubovnik*," was all she said to her astonishment.

"*Tak i bit*," he said. Or 'So be it.'

She heard his leather boots on the hardwood floor as he stepped into the room. Blood rushed through her ears, and she fainted.

Tatiana was sick from work the next two days. Angie had tried to get in touch the first day, but when the machine picked up, she had decided to give Tatiana her privacy. Rae-Ann had been busy but went to Tatiana's door on the second day and found it locked, which she surely reported back to the others.

Tatiana called later to say that she'd been sleeping and had been under the weather. Eyes were transfixed and jaws agape when Tatiana returned to work on the third day, so drastic was her transformation. It wasn't quite what Angie had in mind, but she found herself impressed, nonetheless. There were certainly no giggles taking place amidst the secretarial pool.

No one had ever seen Tatiana's hair down. It was waist-length and full, dirty blonde with highlighted streaks. It had a bright luster to it. She sported fashionable glasses with thin dark frames; they contrasted beautifully to her pale skin.

Her clothing made the boldest statement. Some felt its power instantly; for others it would take getting used to.

No one could deny the stark effectiveness. Tatiana was in a tailored dark pinstriped suit. The tapered pants melded into sleek black boots. She wore a white blouse and tie, but the coat was the most striking feature. It was a frock which narrowed at the waist then widened, ending at the knee.

Angie had her hands over her mouth, which had formed into a permanent smile. She was about to shower her boss with compliments, but Tatiana spoke first.

"Angie, please bring me everything we have on Lumos. I'm a bit behind. Oh, and please invite Stephen Reilly to join me, if he has a moment." That said, she strutted into her office and closed the door.

"Uh…yes…ma'am?" Angie said, flabbergasted that her friend had not made eye contact.

When Angie ushered Stephen in an hour later, he looked a bit nervous.

"Stephen. Thanks for seeing me on such short notice. I promise to be brief. Can we get you anything?" Tatiana said.

He declined.

Angie tried once again to catch Tatiana's eye and smile, but she was merely dismissed.

There was a long silence as Stephen stood there awkwardly. He was shyer than Tatiana had expected.

"Tatiana," he began, no longer able to bear the discomfort. "You look amazing. I've wanted to tell you since you arrived today. It's quite unique, but I really must say, the look is good for you. I'm astounded at the change."

"Well, thank you, sir." Tatiana smiled more broadly than Angie had ever seen. She was radiant. "I'm going to be honest, Stephen. I didn't ask you here for business reasons. I'm going to get right to the point."

She paced as she spoke, removing her glasses and carrying them pinched between her fingers. She moved close to him, her scent obviously tantalizing to him. "I think you know I've been interested in you for quite some time." She leaned in and looked up at him, her forehead nearly touching his lips.

He was trying to stay professional. "I…I have noticed you looking at me at times."

"Yes, that's true," she continued. "I've been remiss, though. I've never told you, after the account meetings, how brilliant I think you are."

"Really?" He sounded surprised, almost childlike.

"Yes," she said, continuing to stare up into his eyes. "And it wouldn't be right for me to go on without telling you how handsome I think you are."

"That's... You're very kind," he said quietly.

"My God." She smiled again. "You don't know how handsome you are. How charming."

"Uh," was all he could say, and he smiled shyly. He was more adorable than her wildest dreams.

"Stephen, please have dinner with me tomorrow night," she proffered. "You pick the place and I'll meet you. It will be my treat."

He looked her in the eye now, like he was seeing her for the first time. "That would be lovely," he said.

"Good," she said, backing away and breaking the spell. "Please let Angie know the time and place, and I promise I'll be on time."

"Uh, right," he said, and turned to leave.

"So, there's no fiancée in the Hamptons, I guess," she said.

He turned back. "I'm sorry?"

"I said, so I guess you aren't seeing anyone."

"Uh, no. No, I'm not." He smiled at her. He had wonderful dimples.

"Good," she said, and their eyes met and held for a long moment.

Rae-Ann came by that evening, and Tatiana's door was open. She didn't call out because she heard voices coming from Tatiana's room. She was going to go but thought she should at least see how Tatiana felt. As she neared the bedroom, she could better make out what they were saying.

"I swear, Grischa, you don't act like much of a *monakh*," Tatiana said.

"Hi," Rae-Ann said as she entered the room. It surprised her that no one else was there. Tatiana sat on the bed alone, facing her night table, still in her work outfit.

"Rae!" Tatiana shrieked, sounding both frightened and angry.

"Whoa, sorry if I startled you. You look really sharp, girl. Good for you."

Tatiana smiled weakly.

"Oh, thanks, Rae. I'm trying something different."

"Well, yeah, that's certainly different. I like it, though. It looks good, Tatiana." Rae tried to act like nothing unusual had just happened. "Honey, who were you talking to?"

"Oh, I was just playing around, talking to Father Grigori."

Rae-Ann chuckled and looked sideways at Tatiana. "Ooh…kaay," she said.

"I think of him as a sort of patron saint," Tatiana explained. "I've always…talked to him. He comforts me." She never looked at Rae-Ann, just continued to stare straight ahead.

"Hey, listen; it's none of my business. I'm sorry I snuck up on you." Rae-Ann felt ill at ease, like something was terribly wrong. Physically, Tatiana looked fine, but she seemed different, in more than just her fashion sense.

"We think maybe you should knock from now on," Tatiana said.

Tatiana and Stephen had a wonderful dinner. He had settled on a little Indian place in the Village and insisted they both dress comfortably. Under her coat, she wore a purple lace cardigan which tied once in the front over a white blouse and a tight pair of light blue jeans. Amongst all the new things he noticed about her, he couldn't get over the beauty and majesty of her posterior. He tried not to let her catch him staring at it throughout the evening, but she did a couple of times. Rather than embarrass him though, she made a joke of it by thrusting it at him, letting him enjoy further. It was a tremendous turn on.

After dinner, she dragged him to a showing of *Eastern Promises*, though it was her third time seeing it. He thought it was really good, and the Russian themes added to the romance of the evening for him. He'd never spent much time with her; she certainly never spoke in meetings, and as she went on at dinner about her love for collecting (including her latest acquisition), he was captivated.

"You're serious. You have his penis?"

"Rasputin was undeniably a holy man, but his charisma was such that women threw themselves at him," Tatiana explained between bites. "My grandmother told a story about this woman who helped Rasputin's daughter write her autobiography. The ghost writer was summoned to the house of an old noblewoman who was still alive from the Romanov days. This was in the 1970s, I believe.

"Well, of course she wanted to interview the woman; it was a real find to have found an eyewitness to history. So, at one point, the noblewoman was talking openly about how proud she was that she had gotten shtupped by Rasputin on a few occasions, and the writer was getting sick to her stomach thinking about this withered old woman having sex, so she asked, 'Do you have anything else for me?' And the old woman says, 'Just the artifacts I got out of the country.' And the writer says, 'Like what?' Then the woman tells her son to get 'it,' and the son, who was helping translate, gets this wooden box about eighteen inches long, with a silver royal crest.

"When the old woman saw the box, she made the sign of the cross. The son opened it before the guest and lying in the box on a velvet cloth was what the writer later described as a sort of blackened banana over a foot long. When she asked what it was, the woman said it was the Holy Father's organ!"

They both laughed and nearly spit up their food at this.

"The woman nearly had a conniption!" she exclaimed, to cap off the tale.

Throughout dinner, for the first time, Stephen could discern a slight accent, which enhanced Tatiana's overall attractiveness. She seemed more self-assured than he'd ever thought, and her confident manner was sexy. They had a lot of laughs that were not forced in any way. It felt right. It shocked him how comfortable he was with her already.

He saw her home on the subway. As soon as they kissed on her stoop, it got torrid. They sensed each other's moves, and their mouths fit together exquisitely. He had ogled her full lips all night as she spoke. He'd longed to kiss her, and when he was allowed to begin, her mouth was every bit as delicious as he'd imagined.

I'm lost, he thought immediately. *I'll never be able to stop this without wanting to do it again.*

"Would you like to come up and see my antiquities?" she whispered.

They both laughed at how cliché the line sounded, but she never pulled away, and her breath going into his hungry mouth as she giggled drove him wild. They practically ran up the stairs and through her door; he never fully took his hands off her. As they headed to the bedroom, they threw off their coats, sweaters, and shirts. She ran ahead and lit a few candles, then grabbed a remote and clicked on the stereo.

He was momentarily taken aback by the sight of the glass-encased member. "God, so that's it, huh?" He felt a bit inadequate suddenly.

"Yes, that's it." She moved quickly to his arms and kissed him, as if not wanting to lose the momentum.

She stood next to the bed with her back against him and lifted her hair, inviting him to unsnap her bra. He couldn't help but gorge himself on her neck, and as he slid his hands under the loosened cups of the lingerie, he felt her breasts. He pinched the nipples hard between his fingers and she shivered.

"You're making me wet," she moaned.

It turned him on to no end to hear her talk like that, and he began to involuntarily breathe heavily. "More," he said, "please."

"I can feel how hard you are." She leaned her head back to kiss him sideways.

He put his hand roughly on the side of her face as he slid his tongue into her mouth. It was so sensual he started feeling dizzy. He had never been with a woman with such power over him.

She took a step forward, and as she labored to slide her jeans down, her hips wiggled, exciting him even more. Her ass was everything he'd imagined and seeing her with nothing but a black thong was possibly the most beautiful sight of his life.

He dropped to his knees and pushed it aside; he couldn't wait any longer. He thrust his tongue toward her and as he licked, she had to fall forward on the bed to steady herself. She arched her back to give him perfect access and moaned loudly as his mouth made contact. She practically controlled his performance by moving her hips up and down to signal where she wanted to be kissed.

Throughout their lovemaking, he sighed without restraint at each new touch. As she first took him in her mouth. As she mounted him and began thrusting back and forth. He had never been with a woman who took such an active part in the process. He had been saddled with inexperienced debutantes who'd lay there making him do all the work.

At each new effort, she eventually sang out his name in orgasm. He was filled with profound joy to please her so, and they spent nearly an hour at one point just kissing sensuously and letting their hands wander. Their movements took on the slow rhythm of the meditative music that played.

As she rode atop him for what seemed the fifth time, their fingers intertwined in meaningful connection. At that moment, he could actually feel his spirit rising up. The weight of her body on him was the only thing holding him down, and he came inside her. He shouted so loudly she had to put her hand over his mouth.

"The neighbors might think someone is being murdered in here," she said giggling.

He didn't care. He'd never felt such bliss. His essence needed time to rejoin his body.

She stayed on top of him as they melded into one sweaty being. She rested her head in his soft chest hair, listening to the thump of his heart. They drifted off to sleep, exhausted after. Nothing need be said to verify the religious experience they'd shared.

In the weeks that followed, Tatiana and Stephen spent a lot of time together. She called him first thing in the morning, having an intimate cooing session as they still lay in their respective beds. She was his first thought in the morning and his last thought at night. They eventually said 'I love you' to each other as they sat on his couch one night watching a movie.

"You're everything I've ever dreamed could be possible in life," he said. "I've never met anyone like you. I don't see many women. I don't want to sound full of myself, but many are intimidated by my looks, or for the same reason, I'm approached by many shallow people. I rarely approach anyone; no one is of interest to me. There's something…a quality behind your eyes that I've never encountered. It's a knowing…like your soul is so much older than you are."

They both were slouched down, leaning back with their heads in the middle of a cushion. She smiled and listened intently, with her hand on his cheek.

"I've been really hurt on occasion," he continued. "I've actually been quite lonely here in the city. Sometimes the loneliness is just unbearable."

She put both her hands around his face and looked fiercely into his eyes.

"Darling," she said. "Now, you listen closely to me. I would never, ever hurt you. We belong to each other now; I'm yours. I promise you will never be lonely again."

Tears of joy welled up in him, and she pressed him like a child against her chest.

Soon she brought a toothbrush to his apartment. They were hanging out in his study, and as he typed on the computer, she sat on his lap, put her arms around him, and snuggled her face into his neck. Most of the objets d'art on the walls were things she had gotten for him on their forays into the country. This was his space, and she seemed happy here.

"Honey, there's something I want to discuss with you," he said. "Something I've felt badly about."

She raised her head to look at him.

"The old man told me to take a crack at Lumos. He said he…wasn't sure if you'd deliver. I tried to protest, but he told me I needed to put business over my feelings at the office."

She remained silent and slid off his lap and into the easy chair next to the desk.

"Look, babe," Stephen went on. He held a red folder in his hand he had gotten off the desk. "You are the most exciting and important thing that has ever happened to me. Say the word and I will burn all the ideas in here. I don't even care if I have to go to another firm. It's not a bad idea to work apart anyway with the direction we're headed."

"No, Steve," she finally said. "It doesn't matter in the least that we should compete. What we are at work is not who we are. My heart hasn't been in it for quite some time, and I've even thought it was the wrong fit for me. I think I'm destined for something else. Let's just let it play out, and if you get the account over me, fine. Don't give it another thought, darling. You've already gotten the girl."

He smiled in relief and leaned over to kiss her deeply. She moved the folder from his hand to the desk as she climbed back into his lap.

Stephen couldn't have predicted that a few months later he'd be despondent and void of any interest in life. Tatiana's affections, her entire personality, had turned on a dime.

She had become convinced that her job was in dire jeopardy, and that to be fired would bring shame not only upon her but upon her uncle, who had been so instrumental in championing her appointment. Though she didn't wholly blame her relationship with Stephen, she more than implied that they should not be seen together until the 'inquisition' was at an end. On the few occasions he saw her, she had started out somewhat loving, telling him they must keep a public profile of being no more than friends, though they would know differently in their minds and hearts.

On those occasions, however, he already knew something was afoot, though he refused to believe it and had in no way prepared himself for the onslaught of misery that was about to occur. He casually asked her to remain calm and not to throw everything out the window because of her suspicions. At that time, she promised she wouldn't, but in the days to come, she proceeded to do that very thing.

When they were alone, she behaved differently toward him, and he felt as if they were forever being watched. She wouldn't hold him or linger in his arms, and worse, she wouldn't kiss him like a lover, wouldn't open her mouth or allow his tongue past her lips. This hit him hardest of all, as he had formed a deep physical reliance upon her affections, having been void of romantic companionship for so long. His attraction toward her was so strong that he could barely be in her presence without wanting to ravish her.

At first, she seemed thrilled and amused by this attention, and encouraged him wholeheartedly, but gradually remonstrations of his public intimacies turned to flat out refusals to embrace or caress each other even in private.

One day, with the door closed in her office, he confronted her after she behaved as if he were trying to rape her when he merely approached to kiss her.

"I knew it," he said. "I knew you'd make some sort of determination not to kiss me properly. I'm sorry to force the issue, but I had to see if I was right. Why are you treating me like this?" He tried to soften his approach, realizing he sounded too aggressive and desperate. "Darling, we're lovers, it's okay—"

"So, I should risk losing everything so you can *put your tongue in my mouth?*" she said with such ferocity that he felt literally spit upon.

His insides churned with nausea; he saw the world crumbling around him. There was none of the closeness, none of their connection in her voice. The spark in her eyes had dulled; in fact, she barely looked at him. She was turning on him. His heart had been set that she was *the one*, he was certain of it. He never would have believed this could happen to them. The kiss was less important suddenly than the realization that he was alone again and would remain so for the near future.

Intense pain at her absence gave way to grief, then anger, then finally utter despair, and numbness. She said that reality had interceded, and fantasy land was over for the moment. Tatiana chided him for submitting to the emotional when she was in 'business mode.' She seemed to relish pointing out their differences now as much as she had embraced their oneness when they were falling in love. It was this pissing on the things that had meant so much to him that hurt the most.

"How can you be so heartless?" he asked one day in resignation. "What about all the things you've promised, all that you've said?"

"I guess I meant them *at the time*," came the half-hearted reply. It was a twist of the knife.

Whenever things were at their bleakest—and he was certain this was the big brush-off—it would occur to him that despite the abuse and the silence, she still *did* call at some point. She was, somewhere deep down, reticent to sever ties. He convinced himself that something of the woman he had fallen for remained in her, and that entity needed him and his love more than ever.

That was until a few weeks went by, and even the awkward silences came to a halt. There were no missed calls, no messages, no 'us.'

Does any part of her miss me? Does she even think of me?

When he would ask after her at her office, Angie would say that she was under strict orders that she wasn't to be disturbed. As much as Tatiana insisted they act as if they were not a couple, Angie was not stupid and probably had a particularly good chronology of everything that was really going on, from the romance through the demise. Stephen imagined that he saw sympathy for him in her eyes, as well as her own agony at the loss of a dear friend who had become a real boss.

On many other occasions, Tatiana was oddly locked in conference with the powers that be. Part of Stephen's own paranoia was the sense whether real or imagined, that Brown had also been snubbing him.

When Stephen had finally been called upon to submit his Lumos proposal, the old man kept the meeting very brief; it basically amounted to a "Thank you" and 'We'll let you know.' The whole thing only added to Stephen's surreal awareness that he had somehow become the invisible man.

Rae-Ann's experience of the past few months had been like Stephen's. Once this new guy started coming around, Tatiana became consumed with him, so Rae-Ann assumed she would lose her friend to romance. What hurt was Tatiana's reticence to discuss her newfound love interest. On the few occasions where she had opened up a bit on the phone, it had been more about work and not at all about Mr. Right. Rae-Ann suspected she had missed the happy part and things had moved straight to 'trouble in paradise.'

Tatiana was definitely not herself. Her level of anxiety over problems at the agency made her sound robotic. Rae-Ann had to remain cool as Tatiana lectured her on these issues, or worse, preached to her. Her kind neighbor had developed quite the judgmental streak, and Rae-Ann had about had it with Tatiana's attitude.

"Your work ethic really bothers me," Tatiana said after Rae-Ann had suggested Tatiana should ease up on herself. "You're so cavalier about work in general, it makes me wonder how we're friends."

"Excuse me?" said Rae-Ann, who was struck speechless at that. She had worked and kept her bills paid since she was fifteen.

"I should let you go. Take care," said Tatiana after a prolonged silence.

"Yeah, take care," said Rae-Ann, not wanting to lose her temper and rock this boat any further. And she hung up the phone.

"This shit has got to stop," Rae-Ann said aloud to herself. She sought out Mrs. Randall, the building superintendent's wife. She knew *Mr.* Randall was too by-the-book to help her in this situation.

The smell of cat piss grew stifling as she neared the superintendent's apartment. The old woman answered the door in her house dress and slippers. She ran a quick hand through her hair, as if that counteracted days without water and shampoo.

"Rae-Ann, is it the toilet again? My husband's in the other building..." she said.

"No, Mrs. Randall," Rae-Ann began hesitantly. She was more than aware the super would not be around. "I need a favor actually...uh...it's about Tatiana. I sort of...need you to let me into her apartment. I've been worried sick..." Rae-Ann could already see the woman's head shaking.

"Please, Mrs. Randall, if I could just see that Tatiana's all right. I know she's been seeing some guy, and I think they may have broken up. That girl has not been herself for weeks."

An awkward silence followed as Mrs. Randall considered this.

"C'mon, Edith. Can you help a sister out?" Rae-Ann was trying to take advantage of the woman's indecision. "I promise I'll be so quick; no one will even know I was there."

"Look, dear," Mrs. Randall said, finally, "I know you two are thick as thieves, so here's what I'm gonna do. Folla' me." She led Rae-Ann to a door at the very end of the hall, unlocked and opened it. "I'm about to go to my bridge club for the evening, and Ralph will probably be gone for several hours. I'm gonna leave this unlocked. You'll find her key under her number, three thirty-three. Now, if that key were to disappear for a while…well, maybe Ralph forgot to lock the closet. The shit does it every other day."

"Oh, thank you, Edith. Thank you so much."

"Don't thank me, dear. I'm not here. If anything goes wrong, you stole that key… Y'hear? I'd rather the old bastard gets in trouble with the committee than to take the shit he'd give me. Ya folla'?"

"Of course, Edith. I understand, and thanks again."

Mrs. Randall conspiratorially put a shaky hand on Rae-Ann's forearm.

"Well, we girls have to stick together. I hope she's all right, the poor dear. Men are all shits, anyway. Tell her that for me. And when you put it back, you gotta remember to lock this knob, understand?"

"Of course, Edith," said Rae-Ann. Within moments, she had Tatiana's key and was hurrying down the hall.

Stephen's assistant, Doreen, buzzed to tell him he was wanted in Mr. Brown's office.

Maybe we're finally going to get started on this Lumos thing.

As usual, he hadn't even caught a glimpse of Tatiana all day.

The normally ebullient Brown was positively stoic when Stephen entered his office. It was furnished in the traditional deep mahogany with green lamps and accents. Stephen was unnerved for the first time. Had something happened to Tatiana?

"Sit, Steve," Brown said with the usual hint of a Russian accent.

Stephen complied.

"I'm heartsick over this, Steve. Just flummoxed," Brown began.

"What did she do, sir?" Stephen asked, deciding there was no reason to not cut to the chase. He knew Brown wasn't stupid and probably didn't approve of their relationship.

"I don't know what you mean, Steve. We're here to talk about you," the boss continued. "I've never been so disappointed in someone. Of course, Mr. Holcomb and I agree that we can't tolerate it."

Stephen had been running a laundry list of possibilities in his mind since the conversation had started, but Brown's words didn't fit any of his items. "I'm afraid now *I* don't know what you mean, sir." Stephen was being completely honest.

"Let's not play games, Steve, okay? Please, huh?" Brown looked downright upset. "To steal a fellow manager's ideas, word for word; I've seen it before, but not from someone with the integrity I *thought* you possessed."

Stephen didn't know his mouth hung open. He didn't know much of anything as he sat there, stunned.

Brown studied him, visibly growing more perturbed by the moment. "Please, don't pretend, Steve. It's unseemly for both of us. Your proposal is verbatim what Tatiana has been working on with us for weeks. Professionally, you are done in this business because that sort of thing does not fly. I just want to add that I personally think it is reprehensible to use that young lady in that way. She has worked hard, and her campaign is noteworthy. I would not be surprised if she lands some awards for this firm."

"Sir, I…" Stephen had no idea what would come out of his mouth. Brown wasn't listening, anyway. The galling reality was that he'd already made up his mind, and Stephen wasn't going to get an opportunity to defend himself.

Brown pushed a button on his desk and two security guards came in. He continued to talk over Stephen. "I'm afraid you must be escorted out. As you know, because of the nature of our business, we must be sure you don't take anything with you." He rose from his seat but did not move to shake hands with Stephen. It was then Stephen noticed Brown's eyes were becoming wet. He felt a deep sorrow that things were ending like this.

"I thought you had great promise, Steve," Brown said, wrapping up the meeting. "I don't know why you think you had to do this, or even if other things you've worked on for us were original, but it can never be put right. Goodbye."

Stephen caught Doreen's eye as he walked through the outer office. She was wide-eyed with shock. There were already technicians doing something to his computer when the guards brought him into his office.

"You can take anything personal that you may want," one of the guards said to him.

He only grabbed a small icon of *Madonna and Child* Tatiana had given him. He walked out of the firm with his head down, too embarrassed to look back.

The state of Tatiana's place frightened the hell out of Rae-Ann. Even robbery seemed too mild a theory for what had gone on. She knew she was going to find her friend's bloodied corpse in the apartment. Even in the low light of the stove's appliance bulb and the bathroom's nightlight, the scene was unmistakable; a violent struggle had taken place. Tatiana's collectibles were strewn about the floor. Frames had been ripped off the walls; glass and lamps had been shattered; furniture had been upended.

"Dear lord," Rae-Ann said aloud. She was shaking.

"Tatiana," she said, all too quietly. "Honey, where are you?"

"Tatiana?" she repeated, and now a sob registered in her voice.

She slowly pushed through the rubble one step at a time. Looking nervously around the island in the kitchen, she found dozens of implements thrown onto the floor, but no body.

Rae-Ann worked her way toward the first room in the hall; the bathroom. She checked each corner stealthily, feeling most unsettled as she pulled back the shower curtain. There was a perpetual drip, drip, drip, causing her to imagine a different liquid hitting the tub's bottom. Thankfully, it was just the faucet, which she tightened as best she could.

When that sound stopped, another took its place; a distinct creak coming from the bedroom. A harrowing thought entered her mind. Her fear had been for Tatiana, but what if the killer was still in the apartment? She stood transfixed for a long few moments. Was this worth putting herself in danger? Tatiana had been her closest friend in the city for a few years. She came home to her. She was like family.

Yes.

There was no running out. She would have to see this through.

Rae-Ann crossed the hall and stepped slowly into Tatiana's bedroom. It was well illuminated by the overly bright alarm clock dial, which washed the room in red. This room was more orderly than the rest of the apartment, the only mess on Tatiana's night table. Rae-Ann didn't see anyone stirring in any part of the room, yet she couldn't shake the sense of another presence.

She stepped closer to focus on the objects littering the small table, and as it became apparent what was there, she threw her hand to her mouth to stifle a cry of revulsion.

Stephen didn't know what to do next. He drove through the darkening city and cranked his music to drown the tumult in his head. He wasn't one for confrontation or dramatics, but he tried Tatiana's cell phone a few times. It was to no avail, so he left a message to call him right back.

He played out retrieving the Lumos folder off his desk a dozen times, how in its perfect order he had sensed it had been disturbed. It wouldn't have bothered him if Tatiana had gone back for a closer look. He understood people's natural curiosity and was tolerant of it. Even now, he wasn't angry at her. If she had been desperate enough to steal his ideas, she must truly have felt her job was on the line. It explained a lot of the vitriol she had slung his way of late. He remembered that going on the offensive had often been her defensive strategy in their meaningless tiffs.

Stephen felt a turbulence in his gut over losing his job, however, and he didn't want to go home to pace. It amazed him that his astounding record at the company had not afforded him the opportunity of an explanation. That whole business was nothing compared with the need to put things right with the love of his life. He wanted to see her so badly and tell her it would be all right, that he would find other work and they would get through this. He could breathe if he could only hold her, kiss her beautiful mouth, and smell her hair. She was a mess, but she was *his* mess.

Determinedly, he took a turn and headed toward her apartment building.

Rae-Ann couldn't stop gasping in disgust over what she was looking at. Rasputin's disembodied junk lay on a white handkerchief on the bedside table. It was bigger than she remembered; was she imagining it was now erect? Its oily surface glistened in the light of the clock, and the source of this texture was evident beside it: a small plastic bottle of lubricant. The smell of putrefaction was surprisingly pervasive considering however long the object had hibernated in its liquid bath, a good deal of which had splashed on the table and surrounding floor. The effect made Rae-Ann retch. Her mind raced.

That poor girl. She's sick. What has she been doing with the thing? Does she jerk it off? Does she actually stick it in her?

The arm that wrapped violently around her head was strong and large. Rae-Ann was sure she was being accosted by a big man. She screamed as loudly as she could and tried to gain her bearings, but the force of the attack almost knocked her feet from under her. She tried to fight, but the viselike grip immobilized her head. The arm covered her eyes and ears, disorienting her greatly. When she forced out a second scream, she was horrified at the gurgling sound that intermingled with her own voice.

She felt heavy cold metal being pulled across the front of her neck. As it slid into place, it caught on the skin every few seconds because of what? Some hard, pointed areas of rust? She sputtered another scream as her mind realized what was happening. Her throat was being slit, but the blade wasn't sharp. It was dull, and there was intermittent pain when it did slice—merely pressure when it failed to break the skin.

A muffled cry escaped her lips now as she struggled vehemently. The arm across her head slipped over her mouth for an instant as she tugged at it with all her might. She twirled and faced her attacker.

Tatiana! How could it be?

The attacker seemed tall and brutal. Tatiana's eyes were wild and otherworldly, her hair tousled. A hand remained on the back of Rae-Ann's neck.

Tatiana's mouth distorted into a horrible, smiling grimace as their eyes met momentarily.

"Honey…what?" was all Rae-Ann could get out as she lifted a hand to cover her own neck. Warm liquid escaped her throat, and as she tried to talk, she spasmodically inhaled with a deep wheeze. She couldn't catch her breath. She panicked now as the extent of her injuries became clearer.

She sobbed involuntarily. A lot of blood escaped through her grasping fingers. She tried to talk but the crimson flow only bubbled and spat from her lips now. She sought her friend's eyes to plead for help, but this grotesque person who was Tatiana but somehow not only clutched the back of Rae-Ann's neck tightly. She caught a glimpse of the century-old bayonet in Tatiana's hand as it was plunged with great force repeatedly into Rae-Ann's body.

Stephen walked up to Tatiana's door and found it unlocked; the tumbler was not clicked into place. He pushed it open without pause.

"Ana?" he said firmly. "Ana." He did not hesitate to enter, knew that if they could get through this period, she would one day be his wife.

"Ana, enough of this bullshit," he said aloud. Too bad if his tone angered her. He'd really had it.

"What the fuck?" he exclaimed as the chaos of the apartment suddenly became apparent to him.

"Ana, are you all right? Look, baby…please, can we just talk?" A quick glance around the place told him she was not around.

What the hell went on here?

He didn't sneak around, being much more confident. He stormed right into the bedroom. Not much was out of place here, though he hadn't remembered a large throw rug which now covered the hardwood floor at the foot of the bed. The disgusting member was in its jar. The water was much lower though, which puzzled him.

He tried to throw a light switch, and nothing happened. *These fucking old buildings*, he thought, and settled for clicking on a dim lamp on the dresser.

He was surprised Tatiana wasn't home, which started his mind on its usual downward spiral. *Where the fuck is she?*

In his hasty inspection of the room, he threw open her closet. The sight which greeted him made him fall backward, crying out. There was a human body hanging from a hook in the back of the closet. The head had lolled to the side, the neck appearing as if it had been hacked at. Only a bare strip of tissue let the head remain attached to the body. Everything in the closet was blanketed in red, blood everywhere, reeking in the way he imagined an abattoir might.

He stood and took a closer look and gagged. It was a woman of color. It occurred to him that he'd been introduced to a friend of Ana's from down the hall, a funny woman, who…

A huge blow to the back made him lose his footing. He stumbled forward and embraced the hanging corpse to keep from plummeting completely, his face submerged in the blood-soaked clothing. He gasped as he came up wet, turned, and another blow came to his stomach. Tatiana stood before him, grinning. She held one of her old bayonets from the Russian Army.

Those were stabs.

Pain seared through his torso, front and back. He felt as if his spinal column had been crushed, the cord torn. Confused, he slumped back into the closet, gone. His last thought was *I love you Ana*, but he couldn't speak the words.

When Rasputin wandered the countryside of Siberia as a pilgrim, he was able to find devotees and form makeshift congregations. His animal magnetism was such that the country wives saw minor difference between surrender of mind to God and that of body. He didn't start out by seducing them, but this often ended up as the result.

People who attended services presided over by Rasputin likened the experience to being in the presence of Christ. Women would dance like dervishes around his nude figure, and the ceremony would begin in a religious fervor. Any woman performing fellatio upon the celebrant initially did so in a spirit of religious ritual, but soon lust and human nature got the better of them, and religion was nearly forgotten. Women were drawn into the worship of Grischa's phallus, imbuing it with mystical qualities. It was a remarkable sight indeed, measuring thirteen inches when fully erect.

Tatiana drove north on 9A, to the Henry Hudson Parkway, out of the city. She had taken Stephen's Mercedes, knowing it would be dependable and move faster than her old Jetta. Clueless as to where she was going, or how far, she knew she had to disappear. She was sorry she hadn't spoken to Stasi, but she couldn't risk anything that might help to trace her. Tatiana needed time. A few days to get her mind together before they came after her.

After meting out the punishment to her so-called friends, she experienced a great clarity of mind. She pieced together the course Rae-Ann must have taken and returned her duplicate key to the super's closet. That nosey bitch would no longer be a thorn in her side, and thank heaven she was through with that whiney, immature excuse for a boyfriend. The message from Brown insured he had gotten a clue about her treachery surrounding his Lumos campaign. *Tak i bit.* May they both rot in hell.

She had cleaned her apartment enough that things would be quiet until the bodies started smelling. And who knew how long that would be? She regretted having to leave her prized possessions behind. Grischa remained in his prison on her nightstand.

What of it? I cannot be expected to think of everything.

The sickness that welled up in her the farther she got from the city surprised her. She drove up Route 9 along the Hudson River. If she had lost her mind moments ago, it was coming back to her now. The severity of what she'd done weighed upon her. How had it come to this? She pictured Rae-Ann's smile and the look of peace on Stephen's face after they made love.

What's wrong with me?

It was as if a great fog was lifting.

My God, I've been possessed. I've lost my mind. I'm a killer, an animal. I need help. But no, I can't turn myself in, not ever.

Tears flowed, followed by huge sobs. Tatiana became hysterical. She had to get off the highway. Barely able to make out the sign, she took the next exit to North Tarrytown.

A plan formulated in her mind. She would get a room. Then tomorrow, she would start by doing what had always comforted her as a child.

She would seek out a priest.

She needed solace, absolution.

She would go to confession.

2. The Hollow Inside the Cross

Piety, Massachusetts, December 2005

Father Brett Elysian heaved a sigh as he got out of his vestments. He carefully removed each article and laid it on the brass bar. It had been a tough Saturday evening Mass, the kind where no one really paid much attention. It wasn't true, of course. There were always the older parishioners, invariably rapt, in the first few rows.

It means more to them because they are closer to death, Brett thought cynically, and chuckled to himself. The poor attitude was unlike him, but the vibe of Mass was in keeping with the rest of his week, which had sucked, in plain English.

It hit its nadir when a lawyer called to tell him of Aunt Mimi's death back in Seattle. He felt guilty he hadn't flown to attend her service. But he'd only been at Saint Mark's for a couple of months, so it was too early to ask for permission to travel. He told just the pastor about the loss, then underwent Reconciliation and Communion as a gesture of mourning.

He'd never been close to Aunt Mimi, and barely remembered ever seeing her when his parents were still around. They'd adopted him in their sixties, so he'd lost them early in life: one when he was thirteen and the other when he was fifteen. He never knew about his real parents, only that the Elysians had gotten him into the U.S.S.R., their own country of origin. They vaguely remembered that he'd had two sisters, and they'd always meant to track them down so he could meet them. But they had never gotten around to it, bless their hearts.

There was a quiet knock on the inlaid wall of the sacristy. It was Inez, the young assistant at the rectory.

"Father Brett, I forgot to say you got a package this morning," she said, her heavy Dominican accent and shy smile most becoming.

"Speak of the devil," said Brett when he saw it came from Seattle. "Thank you, Inez," he said without looking at her.

Inez frowned. Father Brett never seemed to notice her, not like the other priests and deacons. She had dressed for the partying she would do later in the evening, with the jeans that best displayed her figure and the tight black top with the silver sequins. Why did Father Brett never compliment her like the others? She liked playing games to see if she could make them forget their vows, but he was the one she wished would notice her most. He was so good looking, with his dark brows and full lips. She was fairly sure he wasn't gay, but he never reacted like the others.

"Good night, Father. I'm off with my friends," she said, making a last stab at his attention. She could gauge his interest by the severity of the lecture that would follow, warning her to be good.

"Yes, good night," came the reply though, as he examined the package. She would have no luck in baiting him tonight.

She turned and trotted off with a sigh.

Brett barely registered that he was alone. Finished with the vestments, he started to leave, but then decided to open the package right away.

It came from a law firm in Seattle. He got the brown wrapper off quickly then tore at the thing until the contents spilled onto the heavily varnished table. There was a small white cardboard box and a cream-colored envelope.

He opened the envelope first. It contained a letter on personalized stationery with the initials M.E. at the top. He couldn't for the life of him remember what Aunt Mimi's real first name was, but it seemed funny now that she always used paper that proclaimed 'Me' on top. It was sweet that she had taken the time for a note to him. A wave of sadness fell over him, reading the elegant printing.

Brett,

If you are reading this, then I am with the rest of the family in a better place. I'm sorry there isn't much money, but you should be comfortable for a few years. I wish we'd gotten to see more of each other in your adult life. Of course, yours was a more important calling than taking care of your miserable old auntie. You know I understood.

*You're going to like the contents of this box.
The cross is a reliquary, and it contains a tiny
piece of bone.*

Brett opened the box. It contained a wooden cross less than
two inches in length, with silver metal on the back that
wrapped around its four ends in the front. There was a tiny
elliptical window at the back, which, though quite dirty and
dim, revealed a small chamber holding a miniscule white
fragment of bone within. There was a metal Christ figure and
"INRI" sign on the front, both of which had blackened with
age. A small silver loop jutted out from the top, and someone
had recently put a leather thong through it. The cord was the
color of burgundy.

He read more of the letter.

*You always loved history as a child. I assume
that's still the case. Your grandfather spun a tale
that the bone belonged to Father Grigori
Efimovich Rasputin, the so called 'mad monk'
who cured the Tsar's son and had major
influence over the last royal family. The
children never knew if this was true, but it lent
the cross incredible mystery and awe. Your
father and I always fought over who would get
it when it was passed on. You never knew your
grandfather, but were you ever told that he and
your grandmother hid in grain barrels to escape
the Bolsheviks?*

"Yes, Auntie, a hundred times," Brett said aloud.

It's my favorite possession, Brett, and now it's yours. No one has worn the cross in a long time; it's been in my jewelry box for forty years or more.

Enjoy your life in Christ. I was against my brother adopting at such an advanced age, but I was wrong. We all fell in love with you. You are a good boy.

Love, Mimi

A tear ran down Brett's face as he slipped the cord over his neck.

I don't see why no one's worn it.

To him the cross was simple and lovely. It was the last vestige of his family, and already it made him feel closer to his dad. He loved it and vowed then and there to always keep it on.

He was happy and energized as he crossed the walkway between church and rectory. He passed Inez who was walking to her car.

"Hey beautiful," he said suddenly. "Do you have any time before you go out? How 'bout I buy you a hot chocolate?"

"Uh…yeah, absolutely," said a stunned Inez. She blushed, got in the car, and unlocked the passenger door for him. But she wasn't complaining.

When Grischa was eighteen, he experienced visions of pure enlightenment. Light burst in a hundred directions around him, and he heard celestial choirs. He dedicated all the work of his hands to God. It was rare for someone to come upon this path untutored, but Grischa had no spiritual guidance or 'guru.'

North Tarrytown, New York, May 2007

Pastor John McCaffrey sat in his huge recliner watching a movie. The rectory at Saint Stanislaus was dark and quiet, the only light coming from the television and a small lamp in the kitchen as the housekeeper, Constance, sat at the table planning her next day's menu. The kettle whistled on the stove. She ran to silence it and then went into the living room to ask Father McCaffrey if he wanted something. She was quite sure he would.

A decidedly evil voice intoned something about an exorcism as Constance approached. Father John was watching *The Exorcist* again, his favorite. The white-haired old priest was still handsome, with the Irish twinkle in his eye. Constance much admired him, as did all the parishioners.

"Father," she said loudly, to make sure he'd be aware of her approach.

He jumped anyway, nearly off his chair. "Lord's sake, woman, can ya not sneak up on a fella?" His brogue was utterly charming.

"I didn't," she said calmly, ignoring his teasing. "That's why I said your name."

"How do I know you're not Saint Peter calling the roll? You know the state of my heart," he said, which made her laugh.

"Honestly, I don't know how you can watch that horrible film over and over, it nearly melts my ears," she scolded.

"Ah, know thy enemy, Constance, know thy enemy. The Devil can take many forms, including a loveable old housekeeper," he replied.

This made her giggle outright. "Would you like some tea, Father?" She knew full well what he'd say. "And your meds?"

"The meds are taken, dear. My heart is covered for another day. Now, would you make me a cup of instant decaf and sweeten it with some of my other medicine like a good girl?" It was exactly as expected. His other medicine, of course, was a shot of Jameson's.

"Where the devil is this young scalawag?" Father John called after her. "I expected him a good two hours ago, at five."

"It is a long haul from Massachusetts, Father," she called back from the kitchen. "He may have stopped off at the Mass Pike for supper when it got late. The rush hour traffic probably slowed him considerably."

"I suppose you're right," he yelled back. "He'd better hurry. After Karras takes the demon in, I'm not long for this world. I'll be out when my head hits the pillow."

Constance heard the word "cocks" on the television as she brought the priest's drink in.

"Lovely," she said under her breath. He seemed in a good mood, so she decided to push her luck with some meddling. It was what she was good at. "Come clean now, old man. What's up with this one? Why the sudden transfer when we've done fine for so long without a second priest?"

"Now, Constance… When have I ever discussed diocese policy with you?" he asked in mock innocence.

"Whenever I've pumped you hard enough for information," she replied. "Now, spill."

"You know how Massachusetts is," he said. "If the problem won't go away, make it go away. Only this time they're making it go far away."

"But Father, what's he done?" She was no longer bantering, as she furrowed her brow with concern.

"Unfortunately, I wasn't told," Father John replied. "You can imagine what these things are like. Let's pray to God it isn't little boys, or please, God, children of any sort. When I asked His Holiness the reason, I was merely told not to worry, that I'd do fine. The bishop knows I run a tight ship and he's not concerned about us. He seems to feel the whole thing is a precaution and the evidence is hearsay. He feels it's more nipping an ugly rumor in the bud."

"Well, that's reassuring," said Constance

As if on cue, the doorbell rang.

"Now Constance, let's pretend we know naught," said Father John. "Give the young man a fightin' chance, and start fresh, shall we? And mum's the word to the congregation. Are we square?"

"Of course, Father," she said as she went to the door. She couldn't wait to call Agnes when Father McCaffrey went to bed later.

The door opened to reveal a dark-haired striking man in his late twenties. He wore jeans and a sweater with not a cassock in sight.

"Hi. I'm Brett Elysian," he said warmly, holding his hand out to Constance.

"Good evening, Father. Welcome." Constance shook his hand. "Come in please. I hope you found us all right."

"Yes, it was fine. Thank you," said Brett. "I had gotten a bit of a late start." He looked past Constance to the figure coming out of the living room.

"Father McCaffrey," said Brett, again offering his hand.

Father John took it firmly. "Please, John, Father Brett. Welcome, welcome, indeed."

"I heard a lot about you from the diocese when I came for my interview. I'm honored to be serving with you," said Brett.

"Well, I know nothing about you, son. It will be fun getting to know you." Father John smiled, perhaps an attempt to put the younger priest at ease.

Constance motioned for Brett to drop his bag. "Would you like some tea, Father? We were just having some."

"No, thank you," said Brett. "To be honest, I'm a bit exhausted from the drive. It's been a while since I've driven several hours. I'd…"

"Elysian. That's quite a distinctive name," Father John said, ignoring Brett's attempt to move on.

"Yes, I'm told it was French, and my family moved from France to Russia sometime in the 1800s," Brett said graciously. "It is unusual, but I've never been told how it came to be a surname. I was adopted, you see, by an old couple, and they passed when I was young."

"Oh, I'm sorry to hear that," said Father John as Constance 'hummed' her own sympathy. "We should do the research. I'm a bit of a genealogist myself, even though I've hit somewhat of a brick wall with my own Irish roots. Try finding the right John and Mary McCaffrey and what boat they came over on."

"Really, Father, must we talk the man's ear off on the first night," said Constance, smiling shyly at Father Brett.

"Oh, it's fine," said Brett.

"That's quite a cross you've got there, young man," said Father John, continuing to ignore Constance, as was his way.

"Yes, it's my only family heirloom," said Brett, holding it out to the older priest. "It's a reliquary, you see, with the bone of a saint."

Father John leaned in and lifted his glasses a bit to look through the bottom of his trifocals.

"Well, I'll be snookered," he said as Brett turned the cross around for him. John stared for a long moment at the bone fragment with no sign of stopping.

"I'm putting an end to this," said Constance firmly. "You can scrutinize the poor man in the morning, Father John. I'll show you to your room, Father Brett."

"Thank you," he said.

Father John took her cue and stepped back, saying, "There's no arguing with her, Father, you'll soon learn. Get a good rest and I'll show you around after breakfast."

"Thank you, Father." Brett lifted his duffle.

"Oh, Father Brett," Father John said. "I wonder, who is the saint in question?"

"I don't know," Brett lied. "Another childhood mystery, I'm afraid."

"Perhaps we could research it. I know a man—"

"Ah, *The Exorcist*. One of my favorites," said Brett.

"Well, I'll be," said Father John. "I don't know many priests who find that film satisfying."

"I suppose it depends on who you root for," said Brett with a wink, and followed Constance up the stairs. He left Father John, mouth open, pondering that one.

Amy Hazinski was chairwoman of the Ladies' Guild at St. Stanislaus. She was happy with the way her looks had held out at age fifty, but too many bake sales had left her heftier than she would have liked. She primped at the mirror, preparing for a meeting with the new priest who was coming in a few minutes to plan the summer fundraising drive.

She had retained the cuteness everyone always complimented her on, and she liked the new blonde highlights Cindy at the salon had suggested. She sang softly to herself as she got ready, amiable enough unless you crossed her. Today, she was particularly happy. The guild secretary had caught a glimpse of the new reverend coming out of the rectory one day. According to Pam, who could be wicked, he was a definite keeper.

She raised her voice in jubilant song momentarily and nearly missed the sound of the doorbell.

Think of the devil and the devil appears.

She opened the door to find a man of about thirty on her stoop. Were it not for the collar, he could have been mistaken for a college athlete selling magazines. He looked for all the world like one of the Kennedys, albeit with darker features.

"This guy is really gorgeous," he said with a broad smile.

"I…I beg your pardon, Father," said Amy, taken aback.

"I say, the sky is really gorgeous today, isn't it Mrs. Hazinski?" he replied.

"Oh goodness, *Amy*, please! Yes, it's lovely. Father, come in, come in." She didn't bother to explain what she'd thought she'd heard, shaking her head.

"And please, call me Brett." He shook her hand as he stepped into her foyer.

In the next couple of hours, there was much getting acquainted and little planning for the fundraiser. They had become fast friends. Amy had not been so at ease with a perfect stranger in quite some time. Brett reminded her of guys she knew in college; he just happened to have become a priest.

The conversation flowed and there was laughter. She couldn't remember the last time she had let her guard down so. It was terribly sad the more she thought about it. Had she become an old fuddy-duddy? With the committees and the kids and the elegant house, had she lost herself? The fun-loving girl who would make multiple trips to the keg and never failed to take the joint when it was passed around. The girl who wanted to be a singer and work in piano bars. Everything she considered her "deep down" came flooding back.

"Charles never really got me, you know?" she said. She couldn't believe she was opening up like this and fetching the third bottle of merlot from the wine cooler. "He thinks I'm here to be his pit crew between brief stops. I mean, for all I know there have been others, Brett. No, no, I'm serious," she responded to his protest. "I mean, I know I'm no longer a raving beauty…"

"Hey, don't talk like that, Amy," he said. "You are very beautiful."

"C'mon," she said.

"Now I'm serious," he said.

She stopped serving and looked at him, surprised to find his piercing eyes staring, making her focus her attention.

"What man in his right mind doesn't appreciate a woman with some meat on her bones? And facially, you can't say you don't look like that same twenty-five-year-old I see in these photos on the walls. I'm sure your husband has gotten too wrapped up in his business and providing for this family. But if that's not the case, and he truly doesn't see how attractive and desirable you are, then he's a fool, and I need to have a serious talk with that man."

Amy stood transfixed. Her heart pounded. Charles had always been shy and unable to state anything so sensitive directly. No one had ever spoken to her like that. "My word, look at the time," she stammered, still gazing at Brett. "I should make us some lunch."

"I was just thinking of a friend of mine from school, a real lothario," he said, still holding eye contact. "I'm a bit out of practice, but I know that if he were here instead of me, he'd say, 'Amy, you are extremely sexy, and you are the only sustenance I'd ever need.'"

"W-would you care for s-some—"

"Yes." He grabbed her arm as she was passing him to go to the fridge. "I would care for some, Amy. To be honest, I'm dying for some."

She gasped audibly and nearly screamed as he licked and kissed her neck. He thrust a strong arm around her waist, and his other hand held the far side of her head firmly. Charles hadn't touched her in how long? Had it been years?

Everything he was doing immediately felt incredible and she swooned. Brett held her up with his arm. By the time he slid his tongue into her ear, she was breathing very loudly, in and out, in and out.

She hadn't noticed his other hand had worked its way down and already unbuttoned her blouse. He had also deftly slid that hand around and unfastened her bra, and her large breasts spilled out. It occurred to her for one moment that she was naked in front of a priest, but that thought was easily dismissed. Hadn't she known all along they were just men, with the same desires as all men? This wasn't the first priest she had flirted with over the years, including Father McCaffrey. In a way, hadn't she secretly hoped something like this might happen and been disappointed that it never had?

She put her hand on the back of his head as he devoured each breast in turn, taking the time to lick all around them until the nipples were raised. When he flicked them with his tongue and sucked them hard into his warm mouth, she could feel herself become wet. She moaned as the eroticism of how wrong this was became exquisitely agonizing.

"Yes, Father," she said, the illicit nature of her words only heightening her arousal.

They stumbled back into the adjacent bedroom with her pulling and guiding him as much as he was nearly carrying her along. With the same quickness he had used on her blouse, he pushed her down on the bed and hiked up her skirt, stripping off her hose and panties. His mouth found her sex and she literally screamed with ecstasy. Thank goodness it wasn't warm enough for all the windows to be open, though the last thing on her mind presently was the stupid neighbors. Let them hear that real living was happening for once.

Strangely, the thought occurred to her, *Should I tell Pam about this or keep it all to myself?* As much as sharing the information with anyone was risky, this was turning out way too juicy to remain a secret.

"My God, my God, it's so good. It's been so long, Amy," said Brett, raising his head a bit from her crotch. He ripped off his shirt and collar, until only a wooden cross hung from a cord around his neck. Again, this image did not succeed in turning her off; just the opposite.

"For me too, me too," she replied, running her hands through his hair sensually. It occurred to her that she would soon repay the favor, and this thought made her come.

"Oh, Brett. Don't stop. Yes, eat me." Amy liked this new freedom more than she could have imagined. Becoming this sexy person she hadn't been since the early days of her marriage excited her. She resolved in that moment that she would never lose sight of herself again.

Father Brett rested his head on her thigh momentarily. Soothingly, he said, "Now, mother, everything is in order."

After a month, Father McCaffrey was pleased with his new protégé. There was the excitement a new priest brings to any parish, but also something more—a tingling in the air Father John hadn't encountered in a long time. Had he gotten so staid in his role that he no longer elicited the kind of zeal he noticed in the community?

The summer masses were packed when Father Elysian was the celebrant; that could not be denied. He envied the young priest's vigor and popularity, and also his fervor. Father McCaffrey remembered when he last felt that way, his enthusiasm meeting with people from the congregation; his fervent desire to serve and to comfort. He used to enjoy preaching to them, but he'd felt burnt out of late.

Try as he might, things stayed the same, the status quo. Those who never came to church still didn't come, and many who did were just going through the motions. Summer was particularly tough when they all were in a rush to get on with their activities, their cookouts and vacations. If Father John were praised for anything, he'd have to say it was his ability to get through Mass ultra-quickly. Good old Father John, his services were just a half-hour commitment.

He listened to Brett's sermons on occasion. If he could fault anything, it would be his over-familiarity with the faithful. He spoke of man's baser instincts, and John thought at times he went too far. But Brett always seemed to know when enough was enough and would stop himself before exploiting people's prurient interests rather than addressing them. The congregation wasn't complaining because Brett spoke to them in a direct way. John thought something could be learned from Brett's approach. Maybe old McCaffrey was behind the times and the twenty-first century Christian needed things addressed that were really on his or her mind. It couldn't hurt to add a bit of spice to his own homilies.

Father John was always confused when he passed by Brett's room in the hall. Whether the flimsy door was closed or ajar, he could hear Brett praying in what was definitely a foreign tongue. It took several weeks to identify it as Russian.

Since Brett hadn't remembered living in Russia and his records never spoke of knowing another language, this remained a mystery to Father McCaffrey. He loved nothing more than a mystery but was unsure why this one unnerved him. Perhaps it was because Father Elysian's voice sounded so different at these times—deeper and more resonant than he ever exhibited, even celebrating Mass.

This first chink in the armor led John to wonder about the nature of Brett's transfer from Massachusetts. Was it an indication of Father Elysian's instability? Could he suffer from mild delusions?

Father McCaffrey had promised himself that he wouldn't pry into Brett's past until problems arose. He'd collaborated successfully with many priests with checkered pasts; he knew that. Several had committed worse offenses than anything Brett could dream up, and for now his young charge was behaving in an exemplary manner. John always tried to withhold judgment on his colleagues. He was well aware of the innate stresses from committing to life in the priesthood. Brett was doing so damn well thus far, too. He wasn't about to mess with that.

John had been worried enough that Brett wouldn't get past Amy Hazinski, difficult as she could be. She was quite a handful, that one. And as Amy goes, so goes the rest of the Ladies Guild, and as they go, so go their husbands and many other parishioners. He remembered Father Barilyk ten years ago. Even though he had been Polish like many of the congregation, once they'd made up their minds that they didn't like him, it was all downhill for the poor bastard.

Yes, God bless Brett's handling of Amy and the rest of the ladies. God love him. There was no denying his looks filled the parish coffers.

Father John long believed that anything could be settled with a little direct nosiness, so the next time he passed Brett's door and heard him praying, he decided he would simply ask him about the Russian. It was a Thursday night, and the chanting came from Elysian's room as Father John passed during his nightly grooming. He felt bad about interrupting—Brett was obviously deep in meditation—but the young man moved from one thing to the next with such veracity, John wanted his attention while he had the chance.

The door was a bit ajar. A dirge played on Brett's small stereo, too heavy-handed for John's taste. Incense burned.

John knocked quietly on the door even as he pushed it open. Truth be told, he didn't care if Brett objected to his presence at this point.

Father Brett was too preoccupied to hear him. He almost retreated when he saw Brett on his knees facing away from him. His chest was bare except for the cross his family had given him. Thank goodness Brett still had his pants on. So, John soldiered on.

When he got a bit further into the room, he noticed something that disturbed him. Brett's face was reflected in a swiveling mirror on his dresser. John could see Brett was quite absent, as if in a deep trance. He kneeled before a statue of the Holy Mother on the bureau, which, along with the candles and incense, was fashioned into a small shrine.

The candles shining on Brett's face heightened the drama, but a jolt ran straight through John when he focused on Brett's face. Shadows dancing across it made him appear swarthy, and his eyes… Father John would never forget those eyes. Illusion or no, Brett's irises were completely gone. John could make out only pure white globes glistening in Father Brett's reflection.

Father McCaffrey approached Brett. As he got closer, for the first time in the low light, he noticed long welts on Brett's back. Father John had seen this before, but not in an awfully long time. Brett practiced self-flagellation.

He put a hand on Brett's shoulder. The moment he contacted Brett's skin, the reverie was broken. Brett cried out in agony.

John recoiled, startled. He hadn't expected this reaction, and now Brett was yelling so loudly that John heard Constance stirring in her room.

"Oh, dear," Father John said aloud, as he tried to comfort Brett above the din. "It's all right, son. I'm here. No one will harm you."

Father Brett continued to scream.

About the time Constance appeared in the doorway of the bedroom, fixing her robe, the yelling stopped. For a moment, Father John was comforted, but then he saw that Father Elysian was in the midst of a seizure. His back arched and spittle foamed at his lips. Father John, who had his arms around Brett, lowered the young man's body to the floor.

Constance handed him a pillow, which he laid under Brett's head. There was spasmodic thrashing as John held both of Brett's arms down firmly. Brett's face contorted as he emitted harsh grunts and sighs. Constance took note of the time, to see how long the fit would last. It went on only a few minutes.

Father John's weak heart pumped a mile a minute. A strange thought flashed in his mind. *I can see how, in very olden times, this sort of rapture could be mistaken for demonic possession.*

A while later, the two priests sat in the living room having tea. Constance was in the kitchen. Father Elysian had a blanket around his shoulders and did his best to hide the fact that he was still shivering.

"It was really nothing, Father," Brett attempted to convince them. "I have an episode rarely, and I'd just failed to take my medication is all. I'll be fine, really. It won't happen again. I promise."

"No need to be embarrassed," said Father McCaffrey. "I just can't remember seeing any epilepsy in your records. Erm, hold on a moment… Constance," Father John called out, "would you permit me to talk to Father Brett alone for a moment?"

Constance was out of the priests' sightlines, but Father John knew precisely by the creaking of boards that she was listening by the doorway. There was no protest to the contrary from her. He heard the kitchen door close behind her.

"Brett," Father John said, more conspiratorial in his tone now, "I saw the marks on your back, and I saw the state you were in before the fit. What are you into, boy?"

"I used to whip myself. It's true," Brett said, not attempting to lie. "I don't do that anymore, Father. I promise you. I've found other means to purge my sin. I swear. But I have always been singled out, John. I do experience…things. I see the Blessed Virgin."

"Oh Jaysus," Father John couldn't help but blaspheme.

"She's beautiful. I see her golden crown and her shimmering white robe. It's lined with gold and silver, and she wears a cloak of the most brilliant royal purple. She puts her hand over my head, and she blesses me. She blesses me and my work." Tears streamed down Brett's face.

Father John couldn't help putting a hand on his shoulder. John had heard of such illumination happening to holy men and women. He had never been blessed with such gifts. Who was he to question the experience of one of his peers? After all, hadn't he caused the disruption by interrupting Father Brett's private meditation? He suddenly felt exceedingly small and foolish.

"Of course, Brett," he said. "She sounds lovely beyond words. I'm sorry, son, for eavesdroppin'. You have the right to pray as you wish without interruption."

"I'd like to go to bed, Father. It always leaves me so exhausted," Brett said in a childlike way.

"Of course, son, of course," Father John replied, watching Brett rise and leave the room. "Sleep well."

A creak came from the floor just beyond the living room, and Constance stepped into view. She *had* closed the kitchen door but remained on this side of it.

"For heaven's sake, woman," Father John feigned a loud whisper at her. "Do ya' never do as you're told?" He had obviously been startled for the umpteenth time this evening.

"That doesn't wash, and you know it," said Constance. "You were right to check on him if that's what's been going on. I say, give piety a call."

"It's all right. I'll keep an eye on him. Thank you for the tea, but I'll skip the sympathy, if you don't mind." Father McCaffrey rose to turn in. It was eleven, about two hours after his usual bedtime.

"Okay, Father Ostrich—bury your head." Constance turned the light out behind them.

Blast that woman. I hate when she's right.

The autumn leaves fell blissfully away, and so did any fears Father McCaffrey had about Father Elysian. Though Tarrytown was in the midst of a dreadful scare—a series of gruesome murders over the summer—the life of the parish had boomed, with many activities flourishing under Father Elysian's stewardship. The man was so multi-faceted that Father John began to think his history may have manifested out of sheer jealousy.

The church's sponsorship of several inner-city kids at a local camp, along with some of Father Brett's teen groups, kept the parish's youth off the streets and out of trouble throughout the warm weather months. This was a miracle in and of itself, brought about by the tireless efforts of the Ladies' Guild, who seemed to be scurrying about the grounds, holding raffles and book sales and other such events.

Father John kept his nose out of it, happy as he was to finally be able to pass it off to a man with the energy to manage the women and keep them out of his hair. He felt he'd finally hit the plateau he dreamt of in his early years as pastor. He was delighted he could say he had commandeered a successful parish, yet he'd barely had to lift a finger to do so. Instead, he read, studied, and prayed, and took a nap when so inclined.

The killings in town were troubling to all, but it wasn't in the parish's immediate area, and the priests did a small amount of counseling and comforting associated with the incidents.

There were no reports of foul play on Father Brett's part from any of the teenage girls (or boys, for that matter) of the parish; also, nary a sound out of Brett's room nor hint of another seizure. The fundraising had outdone everything that had ever transpired under Father John's guidance and had reached an incredible twenty thousand dollars—more than double the previous record.

The pockets of the wealthy businesspeople of the parish had opened generously. Brett seemed to reach them in some new way that John hadn't thought of, and their wives were also motivating them to give like they never had before. For the first time, Father McCaffrey could boast to the archdiocese that he reigned not only over a successful St. Stan's, but a prosperous, perhaps even wealthy, parish as well.

One of Father Elysian's more popular activities was his Saturday night book club. Father McCaffrey was particularly proud of Brett's accomplishment with this one. John had always felt he'd failed in winning the participation of the adults of the parish in such an enterprise. The club had started out mostly with the members of the Ladies' Guild, but over the summer had flourished to contain men and other couples as well.

From what John could ascertain, they had a high old time every Saturday in the church hall. One could hear music occasionally, and from the conspiratorial giggles every Sunday, there was apparently some drinking involved. It was good to see intelligent discourse occur among the educated adults of the parish, and Father John had always believed healthy debate of issues of faith could only be good for the community.

Father John had been heartbroken, however, that Brett had asked him not to attend. That sort of banter was right up his alley, but he could understand what Brett was saying. He felt John's presence might inhibit some of the participants who looked up to him with the reverence of a father figure. Brett was encouraged that everyone participated freely and didn't want to mess with that.

It hurt for a while that he wasn't wanted, but John soon got over it. Since the meetings could ramble on until eleven or even, on occasion, past midnight, John admitted that was way past his bedtime. He had given his blessing and asked only that Brett would run the book titles by him.

They started with the obligatory *Da Vinci Code*, then segued into a biography of Rasputin, of all people. Father John asked if this was really necessary, but Brett exhibited excitement, saying he could get his hands on a number of copies of the life of the Russian peasant written by his own daughter, Maria Rasputin. Theirs was a Russian, Ukrainian, Lithuanian, and Polish church, and when Brett enthused that this man was the perfect example of the battle between faith and sin, John gave it the okay.

The only thing John knew of Rasputin was that one of the *Doctor Whos* had played him in the film, *Nicholas and Alexandra*. The actor had done such a creepy excellent job that John forever after could only think of him as *the* Rasputin and hadn't even bothered to watch the cable movie with Alan Rickman.

Things were going swimmingly until a profound series of incidents in late November shook the parish community to its core.

It was a sunny Saturday morning near Thanksgiving when Fathers John and Brett were returning from a meeting at the archdiocese concerning the upcoming Catholic Drive. The parish's cell phone gave off its "Poppa Don't Preach" ring (Father McCaffrey's idea of a joke). John answered as Brett drove.

"Yes, Constance," he said loudly into the phone as if he had no device and had to yell all the way to the rectory. "Oh, my Lord," he said, dejectedly.

"All right, dear. We'll head right over there. Thanks for the call, Constance," he said, and hung up.

"What's wrong, Father?" Brett asked.

"Well, lad, you're going to meet one of the oldest Russian families of the parish. They come to Mass weekly, and never attend any events; the Zubovs."

"You're right," said Father Brett, "I've never heard of them."

"Well, they are vitally important to us, Brett," said John. "Andrei Zubov, besides being a state senator from our district, is one of the church's major contributors. His daughter, Petruska, or *'Pet'* as they call her, has cancer. She's only fourteen, unfortunate thing. I'm afraid it's hopeless. They've asked us to administer the rites, so go to their house. I'll direct you, son."

When they arrived at the Zubov home, it was full of family. Andrei and his wife, Anya, met Father Brett then made some introductions around the room.

"We brought her home yesterday, Father John," said Andrei. "There was nothing more to be done at the hospital. She may as well be comfortable here."

"Let's go up, Andrei," said McCaffrey. "Father Elysian, if you'd like to stay down here, I won't be long."

"Oh, no, Father. Please, I'd like to come with you," said Brett.

"As you wish," John said, and they proceeded up the ornate staircase.

The girl was in her bed, barely breathing. She had been sedated to overcome the pain. A hired nurse sat by the bed. Zubov nodded to her, and she arose, clearing the way for the priests.

"Hello, Pet. Do you remember me? I'm Father John," Father McCaffrey said gently. There was the faintest motion of the girl's eyes in acknowledgement. "I've brought Father Brett with me today. He's been with us several months, now. Isn't he a fox?"

"Hello, Petruska. What a beautiful name for a beautiful girl," Father Brett proffered, and Pet opened her eyes just a tiny bit more.

"Well, I suppose I'll get on with it," John whispered, then continued out loud. "We're just going to say a few prayers with you, Pet, that's all. In the name of the Father, and of the Son, and of the Holy Spir—"

"Excuse me, Father," Brett cut in. "Forgive me, but may I, please?" He gestured as if asking to approach the girl.

"Of course, Father," said Zubov, he and Anya looking puzzled.

"Go ahead, Father," said McCaffrey.

He figured Father Elysian might want the practice of performing the last rites. Instead, Brett knelt by her side. He reached over and put a hand on her forehead, then prayed silently. The girl's parents also knelt in prayer. Not wanting to feel foolish, John did likewise, but he wondered what Father Brett was up to.

"Holy Father, grant us, your humble servants, a miracle, and heal this child," Brett said aloud with great conviction.

Oh Jaysus, thought McCaffrey.

Brett pushed very violently on the girl's forehead, so much so that her mother appeared like she would jump at him in protest, but her husband held her back. Father Brett made a sudden jerky motion and pulled his hand back while cupping it closed, as if in a suction maneuver.

He looked down at Pet.

"Open your eyes *Malyutka*," he commanded quietly, and as ordered, Pet blinked and looked clearly up at him.

Anya Zubov cried and threw her hands over her mouth. Father John could barely believe what was transpiring before him.

"Hello, Father. What day is this?" asked Petruska, and she looked around the room, trying to decipher what was going on. "Did you cure me?"

"No, Pet. I can't cure anyone. If you're better, it is the Holy Mother who has done it." He brushed her bald head with his hand and then kissed her there. "Now, sleep Pet, and when you wake, all will be well."

"We'll be right back," Andrei said to the nurse as he and his wife followed Brett out of the room, staring amazedly at him. Father John was deeply moved by what he had witnessed and rose, feeling a bit stricken.

As they crossed the landing, Brett fell to the floor and rolled onto his back with a tensing of muscles. His eyes darted back and forth, and he shook violently.

"It's okay," Father John assured the frightened couple as he knelt to hold on to Brett. "He's having a seizure. It will be over in a few moments."

The three of them were all around Brett now, the parents looking distressed at the state of this man who may have helped their daughter. Anya held his legs while the two men had a firm grasp of Brett's arms and torso. Father John took off his black sport coat and folded it under Brett's head. It was over very quickly.

"You'll be okay, Brett. I'm here," said John soothingly to him as he came out of it. He helped Brett gather himself. "This seemed more violent to me than the other night, Brett. Maybe you should see someone."

As Father John rearranged Brett's bunched clothing, he noticed the cord with the wooden cross was tangled and nearly choking the younger priest. He spun it a few times, then removed it from Father Elysian's neck.

He was taken aback to see Brett staring up at him, with tears in his eyes. His whole face and demeanor had brightened. One could say he seemed like a different person altogether, one who was a stranger to John. Though John continued to work on tucking Brett's clothes, he experienced an eerie feeling.

"Father," Brett said, rather urgently. "Help me, please. You have to help me," he whispered so as not to alarm the Zubovs, but they glanced over with concern. Brett was nearly crying.

Father John tried to remain calm and function as if all were well.

"Of course. Of course, I'll help you, lad. What's troublin' you now? We'll take care of it." Amongst the grooming tasks he performed on Brett, he nonchalantly placed the cross back over his head.

"I'll be okay," Brett said, as if nothing had happened.

The three of them looked at each other but shrugged and moved down the stairs. The Zubovs showered Brett with thanks and blessings.

"I've never tried that before, Mr. Zubov," said Brett. "I don't really know what came over me or what just happened. Let's wait and see how Pet does before anointing me a hero, okay?"

As they were leaving, passing through the living room, Andrei stopped them at a large easy chair, where a frail old woman sat.

"Father Brett, please," said Zubov. "I want you to meet my grandmother, from the old country. She's nearly one hundred years old." He dragged Brett by the arm over to the old woman.

"Babushka," Andrei shouted, "I want you to meet Father Brett Elysian. He helped our Petruska."

"Hello, Mother." Brett held out his hand to her. He was staring at her with those intense eyes.

She sat silently.

"Forgive her," said Zubov. "She doesn't talk much anymore."

"*Otyets*," said Babushka suddenly, without looking up.

"It's Russian for Father," Andrei explained, and Brett nodded.

Then the old woman looked closely at Brett. Her eyes widened and she became more animated, actually pushing herself up and rising from the chair. Andrei and Anya's mouths dropped open in obvious shock; would they all witness two miracles in one day performed by this healer?

"Dyavol!" the woman practically screamed. She pointed at Brett, calling him a devil, and became very agitated, sidestepping the chair and grabbing her cane to back away.

"Dyavol, dyavol, dyavol!" she repeated over and over as she cried out, nearly falling as she hurriedly made her way toward the kitchen to escape Brett.

The family gasped, and a few women cried out, to witness this behavior from someone who normally barely moved. Andrei apologized as he and Father McCaffrey hastened Brett out the door.

Father McCaffrey was resolute when he returned to the rectory. He wolfed down the lunch Constance had prepared and retired to his office. She already knew about the miraculous healing due to a call of thanks from Anya Zubov. Of course, there was her call to Agnes to begin the story on its journey around the parish, finished by the time the men returned home. Could there be a genuine Holy Man in their midst?

Father Brett had gone directly to his room to rest after arguing with Constance about canceling the book club that night. He said he'd be fine by then.

"Hello, Bea. It's John McCaffrey," Father John said when he was alone. He was talking on the phone to the weekend receptionist at the diocese. "I really need Mike Milligan; can he be reached?" He wanted the priest who acted as an assistant to the bishop and was an old friend from as far back as the seminary.

"Yes, Father. I have seen him around today. You're in luck as the bishop's appointments are done until evening. Hold please."

He was regaled by Gregorian chanting as he waited for his party to pick up.

"John, what can I do you for?" Milligan said. They got a lot of mileage out of being two old Micks in a sea of New York Italians.

"Mike, look, I need a favor," John began.

"Oh, Jaysus," said Mike in familiar fashion.

"No, no. Now look, Michael, I don't ask for much. This is serious. Brett Elysian… I know you have the goods on his transfer. Mike, there's some strange doins over here and I need answers, boyo, and fast."

There was a silence at the other end. Milligan was no longer joking either.

"No can do, John. I was sworn to secrecy on this one. That came down from Himself as a favor to the archbishop of Boston. No can do!" Father Mike sounded adamant.

"Look, Michael," said Father McCaffrey desperately. "For you-know-whose sake, this guy is having fits and performing miracles, goin' into trances and Lord knows what-all, so I think I have a right to know all. Please, Mike."

Another long silence.

"Meet me at the Arby's off the interstate. I can give you a half hour at around six-thirty. Can you do that, John?" Father Mike finally said.

John knew it was the best offer he'd get. "Absolutely. I'll leave right after five o'clock Mass lets out. I'll give it one of my drive-thru specials," Father John replied.

"You're terrible," said Mike.

"And Michael, thanks a million," Father McCaffrey added sincerely.

"Ah, it's haunted me," said Father Milligan. "I should've done this long ago."

Father John joined Mike at a table after fetching a couple of decaffeinated coffees at the counter.

"Well, tank ya', Johnny boy," said Father Milligan.

"Don't mention it, ya' old bastard," Father McCaffrey shot back, and they both laughed heartily. "Sure an' it's good ta' see ya, Michael." The two always got a kick out of over-emphasizing the Irish accents when they were together. It was an old habit.

"Same here, John, same here," was the reply. "But I'm afraid I don't bring particularly good tidings. You must steel your nerves on this one, John. It's rather ugly all the way 'round."

Father John looked intently at his friend. There was a long, awkward silence as Mike gave John a last chance not to open this can of worms.

"Well?" said John finally, growing impatient.

"This boy's trouble, John, with a capital T."

"He seems so nice," said Father John, preparing for the worst. "And he's done a bang-up job with us. What's his crime then? Booze? Drugs?"

Father Milligan shook his head to both of these. "Sex," he exclaimed.

"I knew it," said John cradling his head in his hands. "He's too damn handsome for his own good. Well, pray ye, let's have it."

"Well, the public line, and the one thing there was definite evidence of, was that he had an affair with a nineteen-year-old girl who worked at the parish in piety. Her mother claims she got pregnant, but Father Elysian and the girl took care of that before it could be substantiated."

"Dear Lord, you mean she…" John could barely speak the words.

"Yes, John. Father Elysian did not do the right thing when backed into a corner."

"Of course, there are those in this country who think they did do the right thing," said Father John, ever tolerant of people's frailties.

"Well, everyone was extremely tight lipped, but privately, rumors came to light that Father Elysian may have been having affairs with several married women as well, and one of the wives spoke to her husband about it."

"Now, Michael, you say rumors. Was any of this substantiated?" Father John asked, becoming confused about whom to believe. He'd found Father Brett to be a first-rate priest, and he knew full well how the slippery slope of innuendo could get out of hand.

"No, I'm afraid not. But that husband went to the archdiocese in Boston fit to be tied. Elysian may have survived the affair scandal, but when other parishioners got involved, the nail was in the coffin. Of course, the worst that happens in Massachusetts is you get transferred."

"But, Mike…I mean…this guy is a dynamo. Didn't he do enough good in the parish to get some sort of support?" John's own disdain for diocesan politics was coming out. Besides, deep down he really liked Brett. The Lord's special ones had been misunderstood throughout history.

"Hmm," Mike considered. "Oddly enough, they paint quite a different picture over there. He came on strong as a leader just near the end, right before the scandal. But for most of his tour of duty he was actually quite unexceptional. 'A standard wallflower' the pastor called him in an evaluation."

"That's not *my* Brett. This St. Mark's in piety sounds a bit wonky. I think I'll reserve judgment," Father John decided. "I've had no complaints from any women in the parish, and my worries were more in line with his zeal and these seizures."

"I've heard nothing of that sort," Father Mike admitted.

"I think I'll stay away from the diocesan method of guilty until proven innocent. After his book club tonight, I'll ask him directly about the women. I've always found that being upfront is the best policy," said Father John, downing his last swig of cold coffee. "Knowing Brett, he just may tell me the truth and have done with it. Thanks for the info, Mike."

"Well, I thought you should have a fightin' chance, me bucko. It's your funeral," Mike said, partly in jest. Then, after a considerable silence, he asked, "What's this book club?"

When Father McCaffrey returned to St. Stanislaus, it was about seven thirty. He was going to get comfortable and watch television until he could speak to Father Brett.

Who am I kidding, he thought before he entered the Rectory, *I'll never stay awake that late.*

He decided to pop into the church hall and at least tell Brett he needed to see him later. The young man should have a chance to tell his side of the story. John should have been upfront about his reservations with Brett performing that healing. Wonderful as it seemed, he didn't want to attract that kind of attention to the parish.

Walking over to the church, he felt bad about this intrusion.

I'll just tell Brett it was high time I popped 'round to say hello to the participants. I'm too wishy-washy with my supervision, anyway. Perhaps a stronger hand is what he needs to stay out of trouble.

Father John entered the building and went down the stairs. There was one light on in the stairway, but the rest was dark. One would think no one was in the building save for the sound of that infernal dirge-like music of Brett's coming from the basement.

Father McCaffrey walked down the long dark hall which led to the main room. "Can't see your hand in front a' your face," he whispered to himself.

When he reached the door to the church hall, he decided to open it quietly so as not to disturb. He was caught off guard by the low light in there. Many candles acted as the only light in the room, with the pantry off the main room providing some backlight. To his amazement, Father Brett and the participants were standing in a circle, and they were all clad in plain black robes.

What on earth? he thought, and really didn't know what to think beyond that.

Father Brett was preaching at the moment. There was a part of Father McCaffrey's heart that wanted to believe it was a special exercise having to do with the book they were covering. Then he remembered that they had moved on to *The Purpose Driven Life*, so that made no sense.

A wicked idea played in his fevered brain.

A few years ago, the parish had built a small control booth at the back of the hall, for the youth group's plays and pageants. He went into the back door which led up to the booth, being stealthy now. He hoped he would not be caught and embarrass himself.

"Here we are playing secret agent now," he whispered. "And at my age."

Opening the door to the booth, he saw that he'd definitely have to keep any lights off, or he'd be instantly seen. With the lights off in the hall, he'd even have to stay low, or he'd be as noticeable to them as they were to him. He felt ridiculous and out of shape as he crawled to the center of the booth. The light from the array of candles lit the control panel before him as he stuck his head up just enough to see the group.

He remembered that when he'd run one of the plays there was a switch to microphones that hung above the floor. He found it on the panel and flicked it, and Father Elysian's voice nearly boomed over the monitors. He quickly turned the volume knob under the switch, but he was sure the jig was up, and he ducked down accordingly.

He waited several seconds. There were no sounds of scurrying to the back of the room. When he was sure they hadn't heard, he looked up again slowly.

"The Lord is with you," Brett said.

"And with your spirit," the others answered.

Why would he be doing Mass here? Father John tried to understand.

"I have a few words now," Brett said. He looked quite the impressive figure in his black robe, which was accented with a purple stole. "We know the human body is the temple of God, and we also know that, after hunger and thirst, desire is the strongest force that temple experiences.

"Rather than repress that force, it can become a part of our devotion. In various Eastern religions, this sort of meditation has been practiced. The phallic symbol has long been a representation of the creative force. Even the cross was thought of as a sexual symbol during ancient times. The organ of the Hindu god, Shiva—or the Shiva lingam—has long been worshipped in such a way."

During that statement, Father Elysian removed his robe with one motion. He stood completely naked. He exhibited only the reliquary cross and, much to Father John's horror, a full erection.

He's gone mad.

It was like he'd been brutally stabbed in the stomach. His heart sank, and he wondered how this could ever be handled without bringing down the entire parish. Certainly, the career of his young friend was over.

A few of the women present smiled at each other, and John recognized them. All seven of the Ladies Guild officers were there, but there were only two other men besides Brett. One was Charles Hazinski, and the other was Pamela Vargas's husband, Enrique. There were a couple other figures in the shadows at the very rear of the room.

The prurient frailty of Father John was giving way, and he couldn't help but stare in awe at Brett's hardened penis. He'd seen some big ones back in the Navy, but this was definitely the most massive he'd ever beheld, somewhere over a foot. He didn't understand how Brett could begin the ceremony already in that state, with no previous manipulation evident.

Brett raised his arms as though reciting a prayer now rather than lecturing. "Therefore, my brothers and sisters, since we are created in God's image, and since, as his reflection we hold God within ourselves, the highest form of devotion we can offer is to love and worship each other. Does not the fervor of sexual experience border on pure religious abandonment? So, I say unto you now, love ye one another, my children."

Father McCaffrey cringed, and horror shot through his body as the rest of the misguided 'flock' proceeded to drop their robes. A few of the women immediately kneeled before Brett and began to fellate him. It wasn't long before the other two men were engaged in intercourse with partners who weren't their wives.

John was frozen with shock. A part of him felt disgust at the immaturity, like he was watching a group of children being naughty, but of course the ramifications went much deeper than that. These were grown-ups with grown-up positions in life and grown-up responsibilities, and he felt utterly betrayed by them. Some of them were people he considered the best Christians he'd ever served. As if denying this, Amy Hazinski was at the very moment being taken from behind by Brett while her husband serviced someone else.

St. Stan's would be the laughingstock of the state, possibly even the country. It didn't take long to put two and two together, and realize he'd probably be held responsible for this. In fact, as John went through it in his mind, he thought, *This is most likely the end of my career as well.* All the years of solid service to the faithful, wiped away by a foolish deviant. He'd seen so many of his brothers in Christ go down the tubes, but he never expected it to happen to him.

Of course, he had to move and put a stop to this. He got up, not caring if anyone saw him at this point. He was going to move down to the hall to burst in and call a halt, but then he remembered that he could make a public announcement from the booth. He tried to find the right switch to make that happen but was troubled by pain in his chest. And yes, it was running down his left arm!

No, no…fight it. Not now. Fight it until this is broken up and you can get to your meds.

It had snuck up on him and was much worse than he thought. He had felt like the whole thing was foolish and it wouldn't faze him, but apparently it had hit him much harder than he'd realized.

He moved to flick on the outer mike, and at that very moment the people who had been lurking toward the back of the room caught his eye. Whoever they were, they were kissing and fondling each other below their robes, which hadn't yet been shed. As they moved into the light, they took care of that and dropped them to the floor. Their bodies were a bit withered but still in somewhat decent shape and desirable, and they gave each other a last longing kiss before they joined the others in lining up for the men.

This forced him to open the mike and crank the sound.

"Stop it, stop it this instant I tell you," he yelled as pain wracked his chest. The sound reverberated through the church hall. "I'll not have it. It's an offense against God. It's an…"

The pain overwhelmed him, and he dropped to the floor, but not before he noticed the participants were shouting and scrambling for their robes. This included the two who had just joined in the merriment from the shadows.

They were Constance and her friend, Agnes.

One evening on his pilgrimage, Grischa healed the dying child of a peasant family. As a token of gratitude, they asked him to join their religious ceremony the next day. They explained that they were members of a Khlisti flock. When Grischa asked about their beliefs, they referred him to their leader, since they were sworn to silence about their sect. The leader told Rasputin that they believed the concentration on the spiritual was impossible when the demon of lust is present. Therefore, they sought to purge this demon by overindulging in sin.

Rasputin took part in their ritual, which took place in a dug-out cellar under a barn. Indeed, as one of the few men there, Grischa was forced to service several women, including the child's mother from the night before. This woman had appeared pious at home, and after the ceremony, donned her clothing and returned to a life of honest care for her family.

Alone on the road, Grischa was happy that prayer came easily to him, void of guilt or anxiety.

The Zubovs got up from their seats to leave the rectory. They had brought Petruska to visit.

"Goodbye, Father Brett," Andrei said as he took the priest's hand. He spoke softly to him. "We'll never be able to repay you for what you've done. Anything you may ever need, just ask, truly."

"I know, Andrei," said Brett. "I will; I promise."

"We have to get to dinner, Father,' said Anya as she kissed both his cheeks. "We'll see you at five o'clock Mass."

"Take care of our girl." Brett faked a punch at Pet's arm.

A beautiful and healthy teenager stood smiling before him, with a full head of spiked blonde hair. She accepted a huge hug and kiss from Father Brett. Anya beamed at the love between the two of them, the obvious connection.

"I wish Father McCaffrey had lived to see this," Anya said.

Brett saddened suddenly. "Yes, we all do. It was a devastating loss."

"Pastor," Constance said as she entered the room.

The Zubovs laughed as Father Brett blushed.

"Only *acting*, for now," he said.

"Father," Constance giggled. "Don't forget the New Year's raffle announcement at Mass, and picking up the new books for the club tonight. Oh, and I wonder if you could please talk to a woman who's on the phone. She seems distressed."

"Of course," said Brett, "I'll take it in the office. See you all later." He waved and ducked into the pastor's office.

"Hello, this is Father Brett," he said.

"Father, I just got into town this morning, and I found out from people at the inn here that you have a mostly Russian church," a young woman said.

"Yes, that's true," said Brett. "How can I help you. You sound troubled, Miss..."

"My name is Tatiana, and I'm in need of help, Father." She cried. "I live nearby, but something drew me to your church. Will you hear my confession?"

"Of course, *Malyutka*. Come to the church at four o'clock. I'll take you right in."

3. For Luna

North Tarrytown, New York, August 2007

Hank Stanton rolled over, which made his brass bed moan like a wounded animal. He hated the bed. It needed a new mattress and for the sheets to be changed, but he couldn't bring himself to do it. He'd kept the rest of the house clean since Luna passed, but the bed was a sore point. It was the only place that still smelled of her, bathed in sleep.

He rolled and buried his face in her pillows.

The tears came easily, as always. Mornings were the hardest, and he didn't know why he did it to himself, but he was loath to stop it. He guessed there was a certain masochism in opening the wound as wide as possible—in hunkering down and writhing in it. As with every day, he sobbed for a few minutes until he felt silly, though his only audience lay in a dog bed a few feet away.

"You must think Daddy's crazy, Donovan," he stammered through the strings of saliva that hung between his lips like a beaded curtain. The cream-colored Lab raised his eyelids at Hank without moving a muscle. He was used to the crazy man talking to him. He'd been Hank's only companion in the three months they'd been alone.

"Enough of this," Hank said aloud and slid his beer belly over the edge of the mattress then swung his feet around.

Every move seemed a challenge these days, though he was only sixty-five and really not in all *that* bad a condition. His loss had simply made him feel empty, like a drained vessel that was now in danger of drying out. He shambled to the kitchen. Coffee awaited him in the automatic pot. He glanced at the unread newspaper on the table from yesterday. 'Hacker Kills Third' the headline exclaimed.

Terrible. People are crazy.

Yesterday had been one of his bad days where he barely moved, staring at the boob tube all day but never allowing his eyes to focus.

As was his new regimen, he hit his journal first thing. She had given it to him. It was cool, with a half-moon on it, but he'd have gotten himself one with a Giants logo or something. He laughed thinking of her reaction to that. She disliked sports of any kind.

It was the way he still talked to her.

My dearest one,

Will this be a better day? Not sure. I lingered in bed again. I know you'd be disgusted at the length of my grief. You always were stronger. I can't help it, my love. I still smell you there. It's where the scent of your body is the deepest. It helps me to see you so clearly. To see your smile and your soulful eyes before me. I can still feel you; still taste your skin. No one ever made me feel the way you did, and no one ever will again. To think that I can never touch you, never hold you or press your beautiful mouth to mine…

The flow of Hank's thoughts was interrupted. As happened so often of late, he was distracted by drops of liquid falling upon the archival paper of his book. It made the writing bleed where the drops touched the ink. He felt stupid again. He was entitled to his grief, but he knew so well that Luna would have never put up with it. As loving and generous as she was, when it was time to get one's ass in gear, she believed in wasting no time.

This inspired him to continue writing.

I know you would be kicking me to get on with my life and start cleaning out your things that are gathering dust. You'd want me to stop all this wallowing, so I'll try. It's just that I don't know where to begin. There's no one like you in the world, and I know you always scolded that I'm not that old, but I'll never find…

Christ, I did it again, he thought. He could see this was futile and added one more line.

I think I'll start in the attic.

It took Hank about an hour to clean enough just to tolerate working in the attic. There were actual skeletons of mice near the traps he and Luna had put up there years ago, so he held Donovan back from exploring their remains. He'd forgotten about that. One fall they had a real problem in hearing the critters scurrying up there. They'd tried taking a 'live-and-let-live' stance until a bold one got into a drawer, and they found a stash of spearmint gum half eaten, the wrappers chewed through and strewn about the interior.

Hank laughed aloud thinking of it now. He couldn't remember which one of them said their mice must have the freshest breaths in town.

When the dust and the cobwebs were cleared away, he started going through the old stuff. He was determined to get rid of a ton of her shit; she'd accumulated more holiday decorations than could be displayed in a single lifetime. Luna could never resist the sales after a holiday had passed. He emptied one big plastic tote after another into a dumpster he'd rented for the occasion. It sat in the driveway, a source of endless fascination for neighbors who drove down Wampum Lane, headed into town. Donovan followed back and forth as he went up and down the stairs.

After candleholders and potpourri burners were lying in their metal grave, along with the plastic totes, the attic became an airy room. He and Luna had already gone through their daughter's old toys and paraphernalia from a few years before Luna got sick. Mindy would never throw out any of her own stuff, so it was up to them to be brutal.

He thought of Mindy and wondered if she had everything she needed for the boys to begin their school year. Hank tried to be a participating grandfather, though she and Rick had moved their family to Tennessee years ago. This obviously made it more difficult.

Sitting down, he took a break because the stifling heat was getting to him. He sat on a low stool before an old wooden chest that Luna had found at a yard sale. It was 'the junk chest' and he knew it had a bunch of fun items in it. God, there were not only relics from vacations with Mindy and such, but things from their own, and even their parents', childhoods.

Hank waded through a slew of driver's licenses. Luna looked so pretty in hers, never taking an awful picture like most people did when renewing their license. His Russian goddess was a statuesque blonde who always thought enough ahead to have her hair done for the picture.

Tears welled up.

Uh-oh. I mustn't go in that direction. I'll be no good for the rest of the day.

Something caught his eye that he'd forgotten about long ago. He pushed aside a rubber Mickey Mouse doll to grab a dagger, one of the few things Luna had salvaged from her mother's things. It was fairly hefty and long; he guessed about fourteen inches from handle tip to blade point. The hilt was jewel encrusted, but Hank's hand felt good around it. The bumps didn't encumber the bearer at all. Hank had thought the jewels were as fake as the story his father-in-law, Jack Maskova, always told when showing the weapon off.

Jack claimed his father was a Bolshevik rebel who had taken part in the raid on a storehouse of Prince Felix Yusupova. This was in 1918 Russia, after the revolution. Jack claimed the blade was the very one the prince had used to castrate the notorious pseudo-holy man, Rasputin. Evidently, Luna believed this tall tale about as much as Hank did, given the place of dishonor the item now assumed. Jack had kept it in much better shape, hanging on the wall.

A bit more rummaging and Hank produced the makeshift sheath Jack had sewn together from a leather kit he purchased at a craft store. Hank smiled as he remembered the display Jack was so proud of in the Maskovas' den, the knife in its sheath, nailed to the wall. Hank felt bad that his family had taken such awful care of it, whether the story behind it was real or not. He wondered if it might be worth anything. He resolved to take it downstairs and give it a good cleaning.

Later in the evening, when Hank was through sharing his fried bologna sandwich with Donovan, he sat around in his pajamas, using a jewelry cleaner he'd found on Luna's dresser. He had a soft rag and polished away at the metal and jewels of the dagger. After the time-killing task, the knife took on a new sheen. The silver and gold inlay appeared luminous, and what could have been rubies and emeralds for all Hank knew, now sparkled. He'd sprayed and brushed the sheath, too, and it also took on a new luster. With its large belt loops, this was a weapon any Cossack would be more than happy to carry into battle.

For the first time in months, Hank went to bed happy, with an enthusiastic sense of accomplishment. He examined the weapon closely as he drifted off.

Upon healing the anemic son of Czar Nicholas and Czarina Alexandra of the Romanov dynasty, Rasputin held great power at court in St. Petersburg, eventually becoming a reputed advisor to the royal family. Several royal relations and nobles grew outraged at this peasant becoming a trusted confidante held in such prominent status. With Prince Felix Yusupova, a royal cousin, as their leader, these men devised a plot to assassinate Grischa and rid the country of this debauched Holy Man.

He watched her walking to her car after her last class at Westchester Community College. Surprised she was totally alone, he realized he had lucked out. This one was big and beautiful, a brunette with large breasts.

He would get them all for what *she* had done to him. How could she just dispose of him, as easily as taking out the garbage? He wasn't always successful, but he looked for brunettes like her; with big jugs like she had. Man, he'd never get over that she had once said those belonged to him. Never.

This was a great walkway. He was so glad he'd found it. It was lined with hedges all the way down to the parking lot. He could watch in secret a good long time, and then at the end of the row, surprise! It was a balmy summer night and, thinking no one could see her, she reached under and adjusted her bra as she walked. He nearly whimpered in anticipation.

Hacker. Mack the Hacker was what the media called him. He hated it. It lacked creativity. They were so juvenile in having to follow the 'Jack the Ripper' formula. After all, what he did wasn't hacking, not in the least. He was an artist. What he did took patience, subtlety, and finesse.

She screamed briefly when he reached out and grabbed her. That's why her tongue had to go first. He kept his tool so sharp that happened easily enough. She tried to babble a scream as he got a good long look at her tits. He played with them and sucked them. The nipples stiffened involuntarily; he loved it. Man, they were ripe. He could run his hands around them all night, making them bounce, but he was afraid someone would come along any second.

There were a few lonely cars left in the lot. He left a piece of her on top of each hedge to drive the pigs insane.

Think of a better name, assholes.

The next morning, just before he woke, Hank had a dream that was so real, so vivid, that it affected him throughout the day.

He was astride a white steed, wearing a magnificent coat with a high collar and fur all around the lapels. His hat also had a fur brim, and when he looked down, he noticed the dagger tucked into his belt. The gems on its hilt gleamed. He felt every bit the knight in shining armor, as he knew in his heart there was a lady he was to rescue. It wasn't Luna, but a stranger. He also knew he needed to do some killing, and it wouldn't be pretty. There was evil extant, and his job was to find it. It was an evil that brought shame upon his town and his wife's homeland.

Is that what you want me to do, Luna Maskova, my goddess, my own? Is that how I can best serve you, by finding this evil and saving this young woman?

'*Yes,*' he heard her say. '*Yes, my love. Find the evil. Find it. When you're certain, you'll know. Snuff it out. Destroy it. Eradicate it.*'

He was suddenly walking into a large ornate church. It looked like Saint Stan's, the Russian church in town Luna used to drag him to, when she still attended. He walked by the confessionals and saw a strapping young priest standing next to a lovely young woman. He didn't understand, didn't know what he was supposed to do next.

'*First you must learn.*' This had been a deeper voice now, male.

Hank had felt it in the pit of his stomach—this booming voice, like Christopher Lee in surround sound.

He was back outside, riding his white horse in a deep forest. As he rode, he came upon a glen, and at the center, near a blazing fire, was a great wizard, tall and imposing. The fire illuminated his strong but wizened hands, which were raised in a blessing. His face was hidden under a gray hood.

"I am your teacher," he said, "and you must find me. Find me, so that you may learn. You will have to practice. Don't worry; I'll be your coach. Find me under Red Square."

Hank heard a rooster crowing very loudly.

"Under Red Square." Then, for an instant, blood spattered everywhere. So much blood. A torrent.

The rooster crowed again. Hank opened his eyes and realized he was home in bed. He lay there for a moment, the knife by his side. He had fallen asleep with it in his hand.

Thank God I didn't roll over on it, he thought. *The damned thing probably gave me those bad dreams.*

He lay there thinking deeply about all that had just happened in his vision. He breathed very quickly, and his heart was going a mile a minute. Then he jumped from the bed like a man on fire. He raced over to his desk. Donovan jumped up as well and followed, even though he'd just been snoring a moment ago.

Hank sat and pulled out his journal.

Luna my love,

> *Why is it that we always get stuck with neighbors who insist upon having a rooster? Yes, it's nice when they bring over fresh eggs, but I'd gladly make the tradeoff.*

> *I'm not quite certain what you were trying to tell me this morning, Luna. I will consider the signs, my darling.*

Hank wrote out as much of the dream as he remembered. He wondered who may be buried under Red Square in Moscow.

> *Luna, breath of my life, I miss you so. I can't take it, lover. I'M GOING OUT OF MY MIND! I need to talk to you. I need your help, your opinion. I miss your brilliant mind. I miss talking to someone intelligent, someone who cares for me.*

Mindy is so busy. She can only call every two weeks. Why did you have to go, Luna? Why did you abandon me?

The tears came. Then the sobs. He ignored the mucous gathering under his nose, the fact that he could barely see through his wet eyelids. He kept writing, furiously.

Luna, please. Please. I can't stand it. I want to hold you. I want to touch you, to be inside you. My darling, I want to go to our place and have coffee and talk to you. Talk about everything and nothing. I want you to kiss me and put your arm around me as we sit on one of the sofas at our coffee shop. I want to call you when I'm not home, and I want you to leave me messages on my cell phone and just tell me what you've been up to. I want to hear you say my name, to hear that you love me. How can I go on? On and on day after day, for who knows how long. I won't make it, Luna. I can't make it.

Hank had a horrible, horrible thought.

He went to the bed and sat down. His hand trembled as he picked up the knife and took a hard look at it. Brow furrowing, he tried to imagine plunging it into his broken heart, picture how bad the pain would be and how long it would last.

Instinctively, he knew it wasn't sharp enough. He'd have to work on that. He'd have to get it sharpened, professionally.

I'm a coward, he thought. *I'd never be able to go through with it, to harm myself physically.*

I wonder what pills I could take. I've got plenty. There must be something prescribed to me that could do the trick. Luna would know.

I can't even off myself without her.

He cried harder and fell face first into her pillows.

Hank watched a bit of news on cable as he prepared to go out for a walk. They were talking about the killer who'd been stalking women in the area. 'Mack the Hacker' was the nom de guerre the media had produced for this particular nasty piece of work. Hank could barely listen to the report, much less understand how a person could do such a thing to another human being.

The world's gone crazy, he thought, in the way old people do to distance themselves from all that would be left behind when they faced their mortality.

It was a glorious day as he headed toward the Church, Saint Stanislaus. If he couldn't find the underlying cause of this dream business, or it turned out to be no more than the detritus of his troubled subconscious, at least he would have fulfilled his required exercise for the day. He had an appointment at the diabetes clinic in a couple of weeks, and the docs wouldn't be happy with him unless he got in some exercise. With nothing to look forward to, he had been overeating and snacking to belay the hurt and the boredom, so his blood sugar had been sky-high. This might help…a little.

He made a quick stop at the local hunting shop in town. He hesitantly dropped off the knife to be sharpened. The owner of Aim-to-Please, a Mister Crane, was more than fascinated by Hank's discovery. The obvious enthusiast tried to get Hank to sell, which clued Hank in that Yusupova's treasure may be worth more than he thought. He was hard pressed to leave it with Crane, but he figured, you have to trust that people want to stay in business. He was assured he could pick up his knife, which would then be able to "slice air," in a couple of days.

Hank approached the church, trying to sort out how he would go about this. In retrospect, he'd probably made a mistake in dropping off the knife.

What am I talking about? What the hell do I think I'm going to have to do?

Adding this to the dark thoughts that had come over him this morning, Hank considered that it might be time to seek some counseling. It was safe to say his grieving period was not going particularly well.

Maybe if the old priest who's always been there is in, I'll talk to him.

He was about to enter the large church doors when a sound distracted him. It was a reverberating bounce, bounce, bounce like a large drip of water intended to drive a person mad in a prison camp. There was a solitary boy across the street in the church's parking lot. The boy stood under a basketball hoop at the near end of the lot, and he practiced dribbling. Bounce, bounce, bounce. Hank knew this was the area where the kids of the neighborhood picked up the bus to attend a local summer camp. This young fellow had either been left behind today or was not attending the camp at all. For some reason, Hank felt a compunction to go over and talk to him.

He descended the church steps and crossed the street. Getting closer, Hank could see the boy was Latino, about nine or ten years old. He was thin, with jet black hair and thick lips surrounding bright teeth. He had beautiful, brown, almond shaped eyes. He ogled Hank with suspicion as this gray-haired, paunchy old white man approached. Hank hoped he wasn't scaring the boy.

It's too bad kids don't trust any adults because of the sexual predators and what not. It's crazy nowadays.

Hank remembered enjoying talking to old people in the neighborhood when he was a kid. The boy stopped bouncing the basketball and kept a keen eye on Hank as he made his way across the street and into the parking lot. For a moment, Hank thought the kid might make a dash for it.

"Hi," Hank said. "I'm not going to hurt you. Don't worry," he added awkwardly. Hank had always been good with children, but he didn't have a clue what kids were thinking nowadays.

"I'm Hank Stanton," he said. "Who're you?"

The boy remained motionless as he eyed Hank. "Gregorio," he finally said under his breath.

"Want a game?" Hank tried. "I can't run around like a nut, but I'll play HORSE or something."

"What's HORSE?" the kid asked.

"Well," Hank explained while taking off his dress shirt to reveal a white tee. "I make a shot from anywhere I want, and if I get it, you have to make the same shot. If you get it, then you get to come up with a shot you think I'll miss. But if you miss, you get an 'H,' and it's still my turn. Whoever gets H-O-R-S-E first is a horse and loses."

"Oh, you mean BITCH. I know how to play that," Gregorio said excitedly, without a hint of sarcasm.

"Uh, great. Let's stick with HORSE though," Hank said with a smile. "Call me old fashioned."

Gregorio's sullen demeanor suddenly turned into a big bright smile, and he giggled. With that, Hank's heart was hooked.

When Hank looked up to make his first shot, what he saw brought goose bumps to his summer-warm body. Someone had built a makeshift white backboard nailed to a pole, and right above the basketball hoop, whose net had long ago turned to a few hanging strings, there was the shooting target area. It had been outlined in red duct tape and it formed a perfect square.

Under Red Square.

As they played, Hank used the occasion to learn about Gregorio. No, he wasn't going to camp. It was because he usually had to watch his five-year-old sister for his mother while she worked at the local grocery store. His sister, Maria, was too young for camp. Today, he was on his own because his mom took Maria for a checkup at the clinic in town.

Gregorio also asked about Hank.

"Why do you say you can't run around like a nut?" Gregorio repeated Hank's less-than-stellar choice of words.

"Well, I have diabetes, high cholesterol, high blood pressure, asthma, and allergies. Plus, I'm overweight and kind of out of shape. On top of all that, my wife died a few months ago and I think I'm losing my mind." Hank had no idea why all of that had come out of him so honestly. It wasn't fair to lay that all on a kid, and he hoped he hadn't ruined the moment. It felt good to state things that way, though.

Gregorio appeared unperturbed by this litany. He stood silent for a moment and seemed to consider the information carefully.

"Well, if you want, I can help with the getting in shape part," he said, with a mature self-assurance. "You will have to practice, but don't worry…I'll be your coach."

It was Hank who was motionless now. "What did you say?"

"I said not to worry, that I'll be your coach."

Hank stood flabbergasted. In his sixty-five years, nothing like this had ever happened to him. He looked at the spires of Saint Stanislaus, and for a moment, considered there could be a God.

"I have to go now. My mother will be coming out soon," the boy said, without having to check a watch or anything. "Come back on Saturday, Hank. We'll get a game."

With that, Gregorio threw on a gray sweatshirt. He lifted the hood as he ran down the street.

Over the course of the summer and well into the fall, the weather stayed warm enough for Hank to spend time with Gregorio. The child was a wonderful personal trainer, with talent well beyond his years. Hank handed himself over to him, and Gregorio pushed him beyond his limits without making him feel like he was about to have a stroke. They had walked around the neighborhood with Maria in tow in her red wagon, then progressed to walking at a faster pace, and then, when Hank felt he was ready, they had graduated to jogging. He had never been able to do such a thing without having difficulty breathing, but now he did it without faltering.

Hank would have Gregorio come over and lift weights with him, from an old weight bench Rick had given him when he upgraded. He kept it down in the cellar, and that never kept Donovan from accompanying them. Sure enough, after a couple of months, Hank no longer sported a beer gut, and when he looked in the bathroom mirror, he could see some real definition in his chest, arms, and shoulders.

The best exercises were the basketball drills Gregorio made Hank do in the parking lot. Sometimes Hank brought Donovan along for the walk and Maria would play with him. They were extremely cute together. He wished Luna could have seen them.

When they worked out, Gregorio would pass the ball quickly to Hank and make him come in for layups. Gregorio would play defense and try to strip the ball from Hank's hands, forcing quick moves to elude him. They did different ball handling maneuvers, and Hank got quite adept with his hands and passing the ball back and forth between them.

By November, Hank could take part in pick-up games between men in the neighborhood, and he didn't embarrass himself. In fact, he was well-thought of and usually got picked for a team quickly. He was astounded that he didn't feel intimidated playing with even the better diverse men from town. It was something Luna would never have believed. Despite her disdain for sports, Hank knew she'd have been impressed.

With the loss of about twenty pounds, all Hank's other numbers went down—his blood sugar and blood pressure. He wore clothing he hadn't worn in decades. It all felt wonderful, but every morning when he woke up alone, Hank faced the same familiar sadness.

My love,

I'm able to wear all the clothing you've ever bought for me, wanting to encourage me to dress more to my body and not in the loose, big clothing I prefer. There isn't a single thing in my closet that doesn't fit me, unless you want to count all the stuff that has become way too big. I feel better than ever, and I know you would be proud of me. I even see women looking at me in stores and on the street.

But darling, what difference does it make? You are the only person I'd ever want to attract, the only one I'd ever care to look good for. What does it matter who else sees me? What do I have to dress up for? There are days when I wouldn't even wash if I weren't seeing Greg and his family. Who cares, right? This regimen will help when I try to perform the task you've chosen for me, that's all. The dreams continue.

The dreams had continued, and they had gotten increasingly lucid. Hank was pretty certain the young blackguard was a priest he had seen currently serving at Saint Stan's, but he couldn't yet imagine why he would be considered as evil as the dream made him out to be. The young lady near the confessionals was a mystery, however, and could be any one of hundreds of parishioners. North Tarrytown was a fairly big urban community. He just had to keep his eyes and ears open to what it all meant. When other signs had led him to Gregorio, he became convinced the rest of the dream would manifest as well.

It was around Thanksgiving that things got weirder.

First, Hank read that the old priest he remembered had died of a heart attack. Apparently, the younger one would be taking over as pastor until a replacement was named. Hank felt badly about it. From what he remembered about Father McCaffrey, he had liked him, and he remembered Luna liking him as well though he was Irish rather than Russian. Whatever had happened to the older priest, Hank had an unsettling feeling about the replacement, who still figured prominently in his dreams.

Then Hank got a call from Mindy, who cried saying that the boys had gotten sick at the last minute and couldn't come to visit. Hank knew his daughter meant well, but he secretly wondered how much of this was accurate. He had felt an increasing void between him and Mindy of late, and it would take some time for her to visit without remaining devastated by her mother's death. Her family had gone about their business too quickly after it happened, and in Hank's opinion, Mindy hadn't given herself time to process and grieve. He let her off the hook easily and promised he'd make the trip to them at Christmas, which cheered her.

Hank called and asked Gregorio's mother, Consuela, to come to Thanksgiving dinner with the kids. He knew they had no other family around and little money to afford a feast. Luna had done absolutely all the cooking, so he quickly arranged catering by a local restaurant, The Horseman. It was yet another way he was lost without his wife.

It all went very well. The food arrived in the late morning, and Gregorio's family came around noon. Consuela was noticeably quiet around Hank; it had taken her a while to understand the friendship between him and her son. After she became convinced he wasn't interested in getting in her boy's pants, or hers, she seemed to warm to Hank slightly. Maria, of course, spent the day glued to Donovan.

"Serves you right," Hank said to the dog when he was putting food down for him in the kitchen, "for never giving Daddy a moment's peace when we're alone."

At one point Consuela took a cranky Maria home to rest, having given Hank a kiss on the cheek to thank him. It filled his heart to make them happy. He and Gregorio went down to the basement to lift some weights, and that was when things got strange.

"Bring down the knife," Gregorio had said before they went down the stairs. He was talking very deliberately and staring intently into Hank's eyes.

Hank got the scabbard. He didn't remember having ever told Greg about the knife, which he had retrieved from Aim-To-Please months ago. The thing came back so sharp Hank was afraid to handle it.

When they got to the cellar, Gregorio dropped a bomb.

"We're going to be moving next week," he said. His tone was gentle but deliberate. "My dad wants us back. He's been living and working in Albany. We all want to go."

Gregorio had only ever said that his dad had left them, and he never wanted to talk about him. Hank knew instinctively that someone had spent a lot of time on Greg's basketball skills, and it wasn't Consuela. Hank's heart crumbled. Gregorio had been all he had for months, and the boy had single-handedly brought him as far out of his doldrums as he was possibly ever going to get. He felt sorry for himself instantly.

Then it occurred to him that he should be happy for his friend.

"I'll miss you," Hank said. "I'm happy for the three of you. I don't know what I'll do without you."

"You'll rid the town of the blight it's been under," said the boy, cryptically.

"What?"

"You have learned. Now you need a practice run," said the boy, still staring into Hank's eyes.

"Okay, sensei," Hank said chidingly, and Gregorio scowled at him.

"Brandish the knife," Gregorio said, as he grabbed an old broomstick Hank had saved. He had thought it might come in handy some night if coyotes ever went after Donovan, who was presently looking askance at the two of them.

"What's going on, Greg?" asked Hank.

"Do it," the boy said firmly. He wasn't joking in the least.

"C'mon," said Hank, who had taken the knife out but was dropping his hands.

The boy moved speedily and hit Hank with a few sharp blows to his ribs, hip, and the side of his face. Serious pain shot out from each area.

"Owww," Hank said loudly. He didn't know where Gregorio was pulling these moves from. The boy had never mentioned studying martial arts.

"Pretend a basketball is coming at you from all sides. Instead of catching it, deflect it with your knife," Greg said. "It's exactly the same."

"But—" Hank started to say, but the boy advanced on him without mercy.

A few of the blows made contact and Hank winced, but as Gregorio wielded the stick like a lance, striking with both ends, Hank surprised himself by fending off the succeeding blows with the blade.

"Again," Gregorio shouted, as he let fly another barrage at Hank.

This time Hank got into the rhythm, and just as he had gotten good at the fast interplay with the ball, he managed to ward off all of Greg's attempts to hurt him. It occurred to Hank how much Gregorio had also grown in the past few months, as the boy's muscles flexed under his tee shirt.

"*Again!*" Greg shouted and came at Hank his hardest, nearly backing him into the cellar corner.

Hank moved with lightning speed defending himself, and he even passed the knife back and forth between his hands. He saw a weak moment on Gregorio's part where he could actually go on the offensive, and suddenly the tables were turned, with Gregorio blocking the blows as Hank came at *him*.

Hank advanced as one possessed, and when Greg finally exclaimed, "Hold," they stopped to breathe, and Hank looked around. The broomstick lay in pieces on the cellar floor.

Gregorio smiled for the first time. "You are ready."

"For what?" Hank asked.

"You will know."

"Who are you?" Hank said, fully resigned now to the fact that he was not in the presence of a mere child.

"I am your teacher," was all Gregorio said, and he stepped forward and embraced Hank.

Hank was lonely without Gregorio and Maria around. Sometimes he would tease Donovan by saying, "Where's

Greg?" or "Where's Maria?" at the window, and Donovan would bark in anticipation of their arrival.

Hank was champing at the bit for his Christmas visit to Tennessee to see Mindy and her family, and everything went smoothly with his flights. The days flew by, and he had a wonderful Christmas, but something ate away at him the whole time he was down there.

The dreams had gone away after Gregorio moved, and Hank felt an inexplicable and vast emptiness, like Luna had really been communicating with him and now she had gone silent. He tried to put it out of his mind during his visit, but he remained tentative the whole time, and as he said goodbye to Rick and the kids, then hugged Mindy tightly at the airport, he held back tears. Mindy had been inconsolable the first night he was there, but he was happy that perhaps she was finally able to let out her feelings at Luna's loss.

When Hank walked away from them, he stepped into an airport bathroom stall, sat down completely dressed, and sobbed uncontrollably. It was only when another gentleman came into the room that he could stop and compose himself.

After he had flown back and picked Donovan up from the kennel, he arrived home at last. He chucked his suitcase on the floor of the living room and headed for his bed. He didn't even bother unpacking before he threw on gym shorts and a tee shirt and plopped himself in.

That's when the dream returned.

This time he started in the glen, and the wizard had his hood off. He was clearly Gregorio. Hank was down off his horse and was kneeling before the fire.

"You have learned. Now you need a practice run," Greg said, his voice the booming tone of the wizard.

"Find the evil. Snuff it out. Eradicate it."

In an instant, Hank found himself on vast, frozen tundra. It was night, and the landscape was illuminated by bright moonlight. The wind whipped with immeasurable force, dropping the temperature considerably. Though he pulled his coat around himself and turned down the fur on his hat, it was no use, and he felt as though he might freeze to death.

At first, he was alone for miles and miles. Then, a man appeared beside him, as tall as the wizard but twice as brawny, with a long black coat. He was odd-looking, sort of a brooding Italian type, but his ears were very prominent, and were long and angular to the extent of nearly coming to a point.

"Balmy for Siberia, wouldn't you say?" the man said to Hank. His partial smile seemed cold and menacing.

"Whatever you say, Mack," Hank replied through clacking teeth.

"Here's my girl," said the man, and he approached a pretty young lady who walked by carrying a basket of clothing.

The vision jumped forward and the girl laid nearby in the snow. At least Hank thought it was the same girl who'd had the basket overturned on the ground. Her body had been chopped into pieces, and the snow surrounding her was soaked in blood. Hank could identify *some* body parts, and in examining the scene he saw the face of the girl. She was looking at him, her eyes fully awake and gazing into his, pleading.

Hank screamed. When he opened his eyes, Donovan was licking his face.

Hank thought about the dream throughout the day. He knew that whatever it was he needed to do had to happen that night. He felt queasy all day because he had called the man 'Mack' in the dream. As an exercise, Hank searched the Whitepages for anything having to do with Siberia. He half-heartedly wished he'd find nothing, but there it was, sure enough, and not far at all from his house: Siberian Cleaners.

After dark, Hank put on jeans and a sweatshirt with his hiking boots. Donovan got excited that they might be taking one of their after-supper strolls, but Hank assured him that "Daddy has to go out for a while." It occurred to Hank that Daddy might very well not be coming back, so he poured a great big bowl of kibbles for Donovan. Hank fastened the sheath with his Yusupova knife on his belt and threw a winter coat over it. He put on some leather gloves and a dark toque and headed out with a sigh.

At several points in the evening, Hank thought he was now officially insane, to be standing out in the freezing cold the Friday before New Year's staking out a laundromat. Nonetheless, that was exactly what he did. He got a large coffee at the Kremlin, a diner across the street that would be open late, but when it got after eleven and he hadn't seen any young girls doing their clothes at the Siberian, he went back into the diner to keep warm.

He sat near the window where he could see everything going on at the incandescent laundry and tried to stay alert. He got into a pleasant conversation with a heavy waitress named Tyesha, who asked him to take off his coat and get comfortable, but Hank claimed he was cold so he would be ready to run out the door at a moment's notice. He also said he was waiting for someone, his girlfriend, who was going to come and help him do his laundry, because it was obvious that he'd been fascinated by every move made across the street.

It was right before midnight when two college-aged girls came to do their clothes. One was black like Tyesha, and one was a blonde. Hank believed the blonde resembled the girl in his dream. He didn't understand that there were two girls, however, and he was feeling very silly as the clock moved past midnight. He had paid for his coffee and was about to go home when the black girl up and left the laundromat after taking a call on her cell phone.

She seemed to feel badly about leaving her friend, but the blonde was reassuring her. The car the two of them had got out of earlier was just a bit down the street; the issue was probably that the blonde was finishing her friend's laundry, since the one leaving was picked up immediately in a big black car.

Hank said goodbye to Tyesha and milled around outside the Kremlin. The street was officially dead, with the blonde alone at Siberian Cleaners and Hank having been the only diner customer. Presumably, Tyesha wasn't alone because Hank had heard her talking and laughing with a cook in the back.

Hank felt badly when the blonde caught sight of him. She looked extremely uncomfortable. *Great,* he thought, *you are a deranged stalker.* There was no way to reassure her that he was actually her guardian angel.

He decided to cross the street and go right into the laundry and talk to her. He'd convince her they were allies, had seen her left alone from the diner, and felt it was his civic duty to remain until she was safely in her car. It was all true.

When he started across the street, he spotted him; a dark figure hiding in the shadows of a small alley right by the Siberian building. The streetlight angled just enough to catch the man's silhouette as Hank crossed.

Jesus, he's big.

Hank hadn't noticed the blonde retrieving her things from the dryer *and* the washer as she saw Hank approach. Again, he felt guilty, but with Godzilla in the alley, there were worse ideas than her getting out of there. She could hang her clothes in her apartment with her parts still attached, assuming the figure was who Hank thought he was. God love him if he isn't, Hank prayed.

Things came to a head all at once.

The blonde came out of the Siberian focused primarily on Hank. She kept turning around on the way to her car—shielding herself awkwardly with the white plastic laundry basket.

The man emerged from the shadows stalking the blonde. He seemed unaware of Hank, whose attention was now zeroed in on him. Hank decided to make the first move and went into a run. The girl screamed at Hank's forwardness and ran smack-dab *toward* the killer. The killer was momentarily stunned by Hank's intercession in his little slash-and-grab party.

The girl wisely dropped her load and headed for her car. This further disrupted the knave, and Hank was able to get the better of him. He slammed into him with a tackle worthy of his beloved Giants' defense, and the two men tumbled into the alley. Hank could hear the girl's car door close and seconds later, her engine turned over. This assuaged him even though he was about to engage in a smack-down with Frankenstein's monster. It was a feeling he imagined belonged to a small fraternity of individuals; he was a hero. No matter what happened to him now, at least the victim had gotten away.

The man easily threw Hank off him and got to his feet, but for Hank it wasn't so easy. As he rose, the man made a last-ditch effort to play things off.

"Fuck's your problem, man?" his opponent said, pretending to dust off his long black coat and have a conversation.

Hank knew better. His training had given him a quick eye and a quicker mind. In the dim light of the alley, Hank had already caught sight of the pointy ears and understood the man was reaching under his coat to the back of his belt for a weapon. He produced a doozey—more cleaver than knife and a good half foot longer than the Yusupova.

The man actually laughed as Hank unbuttoned the sheath and armed himself. "Are we going to carve some Christmas ham?" the behemoth asked smarmily.

"Why not, Mack?" Hank shot back without forethought, and the man's demeanor darkened.

Why am I taunting the Hacker?

The glowering look lasted for a long moment. It was a recognition that the jig was up, at least with Hank, and he imagined the killer was trying to process how this old fart was on to him.

Then the Hacker advanced.

Hank managed to block the first blows that came at him. They were slower than anything Gregorio had dished out but with double the impact. The knives clanged together loudly, but on the third or fourth collision Hank heard a piece of his dagger fly off and land on the cement a few feet away. His antique was taking a beating, and he didn't like his odds. It encouraged him that he was perplexing the killer by deftly countering his attack, but the man's strength was massive, likely increased by insanity. Hank couldn't imagine keeping this up.

Mack charged at him, and Hank utilized the alley's pervasive ice to slide under him and grabbed the killer's legs. He yanked the killer off his feet with both hands, and Mack went over, hitting the cold pavement with incredible force that would have knocked the wind out of anyone. In this case, it only stunned the man momentarily.

Hank was terrified. Hurting this beast would only anger him, and Hank had an overwhelming desire to live through this. Though the love of his life had died, he felt a responsibility to her—to at least fulfill the task she had destined for him. He got up and ran as hard as he could down the alley. He hoped this side street led to somewhere where he could get help.

Hank cried out loud, hoping a person driving by would hear him. Perhaps the girl had gotten into her car and called

911. His hopes were dashed at the alley's end. The Hacker took his time rising.

Hank turned to face his fate.

Mack walked at him with determination now. Hank wielded his knife with both hands before him. The killer's swipes had been way too hard to deflect with one hand. Hank was nearly disarmed in their last exchange.

The killer's steps turned into a jog. He smiled at Hank now, seemingly excited by the power he held over this Samaritan.

The bulky frame hurled at him, and Hank braced himself. He scarcely believed his luck as the colossal being's footing gave way. The man went down, his cowboy boots slipping on the ice. The forward momentum of this locomotive couldn't diminish. He fell toward Hank's sturdy grip and the blade entered the man's skull in the space under his chin. It went in all the way to the hilt. Hank felt the warm rush of Mack's blood on his fists. The huge body grew motionless.

Hank held up the bulky weight with his arms. He pushed toward the body with great force while turning the knife over before withdrawing it. A rush of blood from the head accompanied this action, and Hank could now see the man's chest had also been penetrated by his own weapon.

A couple of figures entered the alley. He recognized one that poked a head around the building hesitantly as Tyesha. He heard sirens approaching. Hank was dumbfounded as he now noticed, as if it had purposely been hidden from him, a stone stairway on the side of the wall. It led to the hill above.

Hank ran up and didn't stop until he was inside his front door.

Hank lay in bed looking up at the ceiling. He had let Donovan come up one night while lazily watching cable, and Hank had fallen asleep without shooing him down. Donovan took this as permission to sleep with Hank forthwith. Hank didn't really mind. Though it plagued his allergies, truthfully it was a great comfort. He was more at peace and didn't cry over Luna when he woke. The dog's breathing and snoring also aided in lulling Hank to sleep.

He thought he'd be restless that night, considering he just murdered a man and had to clean himself of blood when he got home. But Hank slept like a baby. He had helped someone, saved them and prevented who knew how many others from being turned into goulash in the future. If anything, he was more troubled that he had tried to run. He asked Luna to forgive him and resolved that it wouldn't happen on his next assignment.

The dreaming was very fluid and real that night. It wasn't about the serial murderer, and it wasn't about blood. Hank was back on his white steed, surveying the inner structure of Saint Stanislaus. He looked for the characters in his little pageant—the one he knew was ready to be played out. He found them, as usual, near the back of the church, beside the confessional booths. He believed they had not yet gone in, but the steadfast movie star priest was there, glitteringly handsome. He held some young lady's hands in comfort.

The priest could not be trusted. His mind was firmly ensconced in the seduction of this young supplicant. But was he really so evil?

The answer came in Luna's voice. There she was, all five foot ten of her, standing amidst one of the pews looking back at Hank. "Yes, there is evil here, and it must be snuffed out."

A man now stood next to Luna. Hank recognized him from pictures he had seen at Jack's den a million times. He was Prince Yusupova, the assassin of Rasputin. The man whose stockroom had been raided. The man who had owned Hank's knife. He was dressed in his boyar finery.

He looked directly at Hank. "The evil influence must be eradicated," he said.

Improbable as it seemed, Hank had plenty of room to ride his horse full tilt inside the church. He rode at the priest and the woman. They looked up at him, alarmed. He must save this damsel from Rasputin the seducer, the false prophet. It was as simple as that.

He awoke feeling calm and refreshed. He never felt distressed in the least all day. He was confident and at peace with himself. He didn't even sob as he wrote in his journal to Luna.

Dearest heart,

My thoughts are of the young woman inside you, the one only I saw when you were satiated from my lovemaking. Though you were always sophisticated and jaded, she would make her appearance as I lay on top of you. She gazed up at me, safe and happy, and she gave me the greatest feeling of well-being I had ever known. Rarely were you so vulnerable. It filled me with joy that I could make you so euphoric, and I would melt into the eyes of that woman.

Your gorgeous lips relaxed, and I saw the small overbite, a hint of the tiny bit of French on your mother's side. At those moments, I thought I could never love anyone or anything as much as I loved you, and I would never see anything so powerful as the love in your eyes.

I will leave tonight to carry out my knight's quest, darling. The wizard has done his work, and I'm ready. I know however long it takes to be back in your arms, the reward will be great.

Hank studied the small pamphlet that had served as Saint Stan's bulletin last Sunday. He had taken it one morning from the back of the church. The note of interest to him was that confessions were at four o'clock on Saturdays, or anytime by appointment. It was the Saturday before New Year's, and somehow, he knew today was the day.

The Tarrytown Police were aghast at what they found in the alley next to Siberian Cleaners. They worked diligently in the twelve hours that followed. The detectives assigned to the Hacker case couldn't believe it when the tests came back on the DNA they'd gotten from blood samples. They had victims' wounds that matched the knife found on the body. Said corpse, one Anthony Delmarco, better known as Mack the Hacker, actually had identification on him. When they raided his apartment, they discovered the usual collage of clippings about his murders and victims. They definitely *had* their man.

Trouble was he wasn't talking, considering he was dead. Someone had hacked the Hacker, and the murder weapon which had done that deed was missing. All it left was a pretty little foot-long gash into said Hacker's brain matter.

This had Tarrytown's finest feeling a bit of a love/hate dilemma. Someone had definitely committed a public service and saved the taxpayers a load of man hours. But they also had a vigilante on their hands, and all they had to go on was a jewel that had been found by an attentive forensic team at the scene. By golly, this little gem had turned out to be an honest to God priceless emerald.

Hank didn't walk down to the church at quarter to four. He got in his car and drove over. The trip took only five minutes from his house. He didn't want to wait inside the church because he was afraid that one priest or another would mistake him for a contrite parishioner and complicate what was meant to go down. Instead, he parked across the street, leaving the motor and the heat running.

Hank got satisfaction out of news bits on the radio declaring that someone had dispensed justice in the case of the notorious Tarrytown Hacker, and that you'd never guess what had happened—more at six o'clock on the TV.

It had been a quiet afternoon. He'd taken a nap. Odd that his cell phone had rung a few times, but even if it was Mindy, he didn't want anything to deter him from his appointed task.

He wasn't the bundle of nerves he'd been the previous night. He didn't suppose this priest would be a problem after his showdown with Goliath, and he hoped he could get this over quick and get back to his cable. The Giants were pitted against the undefeated New England Patriots that night and it promised to be quite a game. He'd left another vat of kibbles for Donovan just in case.

It was only minutes before he saw the young priest make his way across the rectory lawn. The man was rugged and handsome; he had to give him that. Hank had studied the bulletin thoroughly. The acting pastor was Father Brett Elysian. He wondered what immutable crime this holy man could have committed. Could he have had some undiscovered culpability in the death of the previous pastor, McCaffrey? Was he skimming off the top of the collection basket, Hank wondered?

Without missing a beat, another car pulled up. At first, the driver seemed intent upon parking in front of the church, but Hank guessed it became apparent how narrow the street was and the car pulled into the lot. Hank hadn't expected this, and for a moment he nearly ducked down in his seat but instead sat calmly as if waiting for someone to emerge from the church.

When her car was settled into the very spot next to Hank's, the young driver looked over at him briefly. Hank felt a rush of panic as their eyes met. She was the woman from his dream down to every last hair on her head. In real life she seemed more demure.

With all the supernatural events surrounding him for months, would the young lady ferret out the truth of what was about to take place? For a moment, Hank wished it so, that she would sense some danger, get back in her car, and drive far away. Then he could go home and live his life and try to reconcile his losses one last time. He even thought of jumping out and attempting to keep her from meeting the priest, but he realized he'd sound like a madman. But maybe that would be enough to make her flee the scene.

As each of these scenarios presented themselves, she gave him a quick smile, got out of her car, and crossed the street into the church. Hank realized beyond hope that things would play out as foretold. There was no reason to delay at this point, so Hank got out of the car and made his way across the street.

Lieutenant Stern, assigned to the Hacker case, had been blessed with great insight. He was a rugged outdoorsman, a John Wayne type, who when not in his suit for work, could usually be found in a flannel shirt and Mets hat. He collected swords and weapons, and he believed the jewel in question had popped off the hilt or scabbard of whatever had invaded the cranium of Tarrytown's own Ripper, Mister Delmarco.

The indefatigable Stern took a chance and called upon the haunts of local sportsmen for a start, to see if anyone had come across a blade more than a foot long that may have had its share of bling attached. There weren't that many establishments to go through.

Bingo, his day was made when he came across a Mister Crane at Aim-to-Please, a gun and hobby shop. Not only had the proprietor seen such a weapon, but he had also serviced it for a gentleman by the name of H. Stanton who had walked there from the neighborhood. He had only a telephone number. It didn't take much for Crane to realize that he had sharpened the blade that brought down Mack the Hacker. The man just about danced the "Macarena" as the cops left.

Stern had tried the phone a few times at Stanton's but got no answer. He needed a little while to correlate that Crane's description of the man perfectly matched those of a waitress and a college student from the scene the night before. He was on a roll and felt someone up there may have been interceding in his investigation. Things rarely came together in this way.

When he did a reverse telephone number search on the internet's Whitepages, Stern got a squad together and rushed over to the Wampum Lane address. He was dejected Stanton wasn't at home, but some neighbors collecting eggs in their backyard said they'd seen him take off in his car not long ago. They said that to their knowledge, Mr. Stanton never went far. He was almost always home. They gave a thorough description of the car; Stern had already gotten the plate number through the DMV. With that, the caravan was off in search of Hank's white '97 Honda Civic.

They drove by local landmarks such as the grocery store and neighborhood drug store, and Stern's incredible streak held up as they spotted the Civic parked outside the church where Stanton attended, St. Stanislaus. Lieutenant Stern made the sign of the cross as the cruisers pulled up, lights flashing. Divine providence had surely done his work for him today.

Hank had entered the church to find the pair in the exact positions they had occupied in the dream. Father Elysian was comforting the young lady. Her tears flowed, and he had both her hands in his. Since Hank had followed her in, he knew they hadn't made it into one of the confessionals, though that surely had been the plan.

He walked in their direction as if he were the next penitent. His head swam as if ensconced in the dream. Seeing the scene before him was like envisioning that world all over again. He grew woozy and felt the urge to immediately lie down and nap. Hank worried he might pass out and never complete this task.

No, he demanded of himself, *I have to do what Luna came all the way from the other side to recruit me for.*

Out of the corner of his eye, the priest noticed Hank approaching. Hank read disappointment in the priest's face that someone had shown up. Hank was grateful no one else was around. It gave him a moment to plan his next move.

"I'll be with you soon, sir," Father Elysian said. "Have patience." Hank nodded. The priest had never looked directly at him. Now Elysian addressed the woman. "Go on, Tatiana," Hank heard him say.

Father Elysian had caught Hank off guard, and he ducked into one of the pews. Something was wrong; he could feel it. Things were not as apparent as he'd imagined they'd be from the dream. He still didn't get why he had to kill this man, though he definitely sensed another presence in the room. It was an old and powerful being, one that was charismatic and used to getting its way. Hank really struggled when he looked over and saw Luna and Yusupova, clear as day, just as they had looked in his dream.

Hank panicked. *I'm losing it. I have to get on with this and be done.*

He slid out of the pew and walked toward the pair. The woman had taken no notice of him. She was in a bad state and trying to unburden herself. As Hank came closer to them, he became more confused as to what he must do.

What's wrong Luna, he thought. *What am I feeling?*

'*Find the evil*,' he heard her voice in his head, '*and snuff it out.*'

Hank took out his knife and walked more quickly toward Father Brett. The priest was trying to keep up with Tatiana, and it took him a long time to realize he was about to be attacked. Once he noticed Hank, he turned toward him and tried to move quickly to stop him, but Hank was in decent shape and had a head start. Hank seized the priest by the arm and moved in on him.

Hank was getting mixed signals, and when he touched the priest, something came to him. He yanked open Father Elysian's sport coat and saw a wooden cross dangling from the priest's neck. As he lunged forward with the knife, he surprised the priest by lifting the cross with the blade rather than stabbing him. Hank pulled the knife back and cut the cord, pushing Father Elysian down in the process.

The priest fell hard on his backside in the aisle. The cross fell to the ground, and Hank's instincts kicked in. He brought his hiking boot down hard upon it, shattering it to bits. Something small and white flew out of the side of the crucifix. Hank turned toward the woman while the priest remained on the ground.

Hank sensed Father Elysian was different somehow. He no longer felt that other presence coming from him. But the woman was another matter. She had barely stopped crying as things unfolded before her. She had gasped when Hank charged and attacked the priest, having been caught completely off guard.

Hank heard commotion behind him as he grabbed the woman. A bunch of people ran into the church and shouted at him, but Hank couldn't afford to pay attention. Some power emanated from the woman—a force so strong and malevolent. She was not the damsel in distress he'd thought her to be. She was evil, and she had done horrible things.

Hank sensed innocent souls crying for vengeance, souls that required rest. He heard Luna's voice distinctly. '*Snuff it out*,' she said.

Then another voice came, louder and more present. "Put the knife down. I repeat, sir, drop your weapon."

The woman the priest had called Tatiana looked into his eyes. "*Tak i bit,*" she said, and Hank drilled his knife into her stomach.

He heard gunshots, and sharp pain burned through his back and various parts of his body. A bullet struck him for every thrust of his knife into the woman, and there were several. He continued to stab her, making sure to use all his remaining strength and to bury the knife as deeply as it would go each time. He did it over and over until the eyes that blazed into his went cold and glossy.

Until the evil flame was gone from them. Until the life was gone.

Hank saw Luna watching him from one of the pews. Her smile was the last thing he saw before he fell, dropping the bloodied knife to the ground.

On the night Rasputin was murdered, in a cellar room of Prince Yusupova's palace, he was fed enough poisoned cakes to take down several men.

This did not kill him, so he was shot, beaten, used sexually, mutilated through castration and, as he fled the scene out into the courtyard, shot in the back just a few feet from the street.

His body was bound and thrown off the Petrovsky Bridge into the icy Neva River. The cause of death was determined to be drowning.

When the body was found, he had escaped his bindings. Grischa had been alive when he went into the water.

THE END?

Not if you want to dive into more of Crystal Lake Publishing's Tales from the Darkest Depths!

Check out our amazing website and online store or download our latest catalog here: https://geni.us/CLPCatalog.

We always have great new projects and content on the website to dive into, as well as a newsletter, behind the scenes options, social media platforms, our own dark fiction shared-world series and our very own webstore. Our webstore even has categories specifically for KU books, non-fiction, anthologies, and of course more novels and novellas.

AUTHOR BIOGRAPHY

Richard Alan Scott's work has appeared in magazines like *Premiere*, *Shroud*, and *Albedo One* (Ireland 's #1 Genre magazine), and the *Wicked Creatures* and *Walls and Bridges* Anthologies. His blog is the *Labyrinth Project Creators Journal* of New Orleans, and he's featured in 3 CD/Books: *The Black Stone*, *The Beyond*, and *The Body of Horror* from Eighth Tower Books in Italy. He was guest writer for Crystal Lake Publishing's Still Water Bay series. He has two novels that are being queried and lives in rural Rhode Island near Lovecraft and Eddy's Great Dark Swamp. Visit him at richardalanscott.com.

Readers…

Thank you for reading *Relics from the Underworld*. We hope
you enjoyed this novel. If you have a moment, please review
Relics from the Underworld at the store where you bought it.

Help other readers by telling them why you enjoyed this book.
No need to write an in-depth discussion. Even a single sentence
will be greatly appreciated. Reviews go a long way to helping a
book sell, and is great for an author's career. It'll also help us
to continue publishing quality books.

Thank you again for taking the time to journey with Crystal
Lake's Torrid Waters.

You will find links to all our social media platforms on our
Linktree page: https://linktr.ee/CrystalLakePublishing.

MISSION STATEMENT

Since its founding in August 2012, Crystal Lake Publishing has quickly become one of the world's leading publishers of Dark Fiction and Horror books. In 2023, Crystal Lake Publishing formed a part of Crystal Lake Entertainment, joining several other divisions, including Torrid Waters, Crystal Lake Comics, and many more.

While we strive to present only the highest quality fiction and entertainment, we also endeavour to support authors along their writing journey. We offer our time and experience in non-fiction projects, as well as author mentoring and services, at competitive prices.

With several Bram Stoker Award wins and many other wins and nominations (including the HWA's Specialty Press Award), Crystal Lake puts integrity, honor, and respect at the forefront of our publishing operations.

We strive for each book and outreach program we spearhead to not only entertain and touch or comment on issues that affect our readers, but also to strengthen and support the Dark Fiction field and its authors.

Not only do we find and publish authors we believe are destined for greatness, but we strive to work with men and women who endeavour to be decent human beings who care more for others than themselves, while still being hard-working, driven, and passionate artists and storytellers.

Crystal Lake is and will always be a beacon of what passion and dedication, combined with overwhelming teamwork and respect, can accomplish. We endeavour to know each and every one of our readers, while building personal relationships with our authors, reviewers, bloggers, podcasters, bookstores, and libraries.

This is what we believe in. What we stand for. This will be our legacy.

Welcome to Crystal Lake Entertainment.

THANK YOU FOR PURCHASING THIS BOOK